LIGHT YEARS

a novel

ALSO AVAILABLE FROM LAUREL-LEAF BOOKS

BEFORE WE WERE FREE, *Julia Alvarez*

I AM THE CHEESE, *Robert Cormier*

THE PARALLEL UNIVERSE OF LIARS, *Kathleen Jeffrie Johnson*

GATHERING BLUE, *Lois Lowry*

LEAVING JETTY ROAD, *Rebecca Burton*

HAVELI, *Suzanne Fisher Staples*

STARGIRL, *Jerry Spinelli*

THE CENTER OF THE WORLD, *Andreas Steinhöfel*

TAMMAR STEIN

LIGHT YEARS

a novel

LAUREL-LEAF BOOKS

For Fred

Published by Laurel-Leaf
an imprint of Random House Children's Books
a division of Random House, Inc.
New York

Originally published in hardcover in the United States by Alfred A. Knopf Books for Young Readers, New York, in 2005. This edition published by arrangement with Alfred A. Knopf Books for Young Readers.

The Library of Congress has cataloged the hardcover edition of this work as follows:
Stein, Tammar.
Light years : a novel / by Tammar Stein.
p. cm.
Summary: Maya Laor leaves her home in Israel to study astronomy at the University of Virginia after the tragic death of her boyfriend in a suicide bombing.
ISBN: 978-0-375-83023-5 (trade) — ISBN: 978-0-375-93023-2 (lib. bdg.)
[1. Suicide bombings—Fiction. 2. Arab-Israeli conflict—Fiction. 3. Grief—Fiction.]
I. Title.
PZ7.S821645Li 2005
[Fic]—dc22
2004007776

RL: 6.2
ISBN: 978-0-440-23902-4 (pbk.)
Reprinted by arrangement with Alfred A. Knopf Books for Young Readers
June 2008
Printed in the United States of America
10 9 8 7 6 5 4 3 2 1
First Laurel-Leaf Edition

He went to school to learn how to kill me.

They taught him how to carry the bomb strapped to his waist, how to dress so that bulging explosives wouldn't show. They taught him to meet people's eyes and walk normally so as not to draw attention. They practiced what to do if someone shouted, "Stop!" or if people started to stare, and when to push the red button. Always, they drilled, when in doubt, if you think they'll try to stop you, press the red button. He even had his photo taken so that his parents could display it at his all-expenses-paid funeral.

Sooner than he could have expected, everything had been set up—his ride to Tel Aviv, the bomb made out of fertilizer and sugar, embedded with nails, no heavier than the one he had practiced with. He was blessed one last time, and after they dropped him off a few streets away from the café, he was on his own, ready to go.

I wonder all the time if his heart was racing fit to burst. If his palms were sweaty, his mouth dry. If he was sorry that he had set this all in motion. If he was more scared to turn back than to go forward. If he was calm. Or high. Or if he was eager. If I had seen him, would I have known what he was about to do?

But those are questions that I will never know the answer to.

He didn't kill me. I was on the bus, stuck in traffic. The girl who got him fired. The Israeli girl who ruined his life.

Seven other people were killed instead.

A single mother of two. A computer programmer. Two college students. A grandmother and her four-year-old grandson sharing an ice cream. And Dov, my boyfriend, my heart, the man I wanted to marry, who was there waiting for me.

I wonder if the Palestinian bomber would be pleased that it turned out this way. An eye for an eye. A tooth for a tooth.

I ruined his life. So he ruined mine.

Chapter One

VIRGINIA

I thought I might sleep on the bus, but I couldn't.

I was tired, but the landscape whooshing by was too new, too important to lull me to sleep. It was hard to believe this place. Rolling green hills, wooden fences rising and falling in gentle undulation as the bus glided by them. Red farmhouses, silver silos, brown cows.

In the bus's air-conditioned climate, I could look out and enjoy the beauty, but knowing the heavy humidity that hung just outside the huge glass windows made me nervous. The landscape looked so civilized and tame, it was hard to reconcile it with the exotic, nearly tropical humidity in the air. I never felt anything like that lethargy that settled over me when I stepped outside the airport with my bags. I couldn't breathe; the air was as thick as soup.

Slouched in my seat, I rubbed the heel of my palm between my eyebrows, where a headache had been growing since the plane crossed over Greenland. A green sign flashed by and I reminded myself that the distance was measured in miles, not kilometers. It had been years since I studied miles, feet, and Fahrenheit temperatures. I only had a faint grasp of what they actually meant. It made me feel like a child again. Are we there yet? Are we there yet?

I tried to find a comfortable place to lean my head and resolutely closed my eyes. It was going to be a long day once I reached Charlottesville; I hadn't slept in over thirty hours and had a seven-hour jet lag to reconcile. Any sleep I could get would be useful. But sleep never worked like that for me. Unlike Dov, who could fall asleep anywhere, under any condition. He claimed it was a skill, not a God-given talent, but I never learned how to turn a switch and sleep.

I hadn't learned how to turn a switch and stop thinking about Dov either.

I spent the rest of the ride pretending to sleep, hoping to trick my overtired mind and let go of memories best left behind.

The bus pulled up to the terminal in Charlottesville with a relieved whoosh and I disembarked, feeling even more lost and homesick in this tiny abandoned station.

Homesick. That's a funny word. Especially since I came here because I was sick of home. Still, on arriving at the bus station, so tired I swayed on my feet, I had a bone-deep feeling that I shouldn't have come.

The bus driver hauled out my three bags from under the bus and shook his head at the folly of packing so heavy. He climbed back into his silver bus, which shuddered, beeped, and lurched as he reversed and drove away.

I studied my bags. One army-issue green duffel. My mother's gray suitcase with four tiny wheels. One red-and-black canvas suitcase. It went against my grain to bring along more bags than I had arms to carry them with. Then again, this was all I had owned for the past two years and all I planned to own for the next four. Not much when you think of it that way.

The station, with its dusty gray linoleum floor, ancient vending machines, and a sleepy-looking woman watching television, looked forgotten. It was too quiet. It was nothing like the hustle and bustle of the Haifa station, with its huge timetable of buses arriving and leaving, soldiers coming home or returning to base, tourists with backpacks, businessmen with briefcases, the smell of falafel drifting everywhere, and kiosks packed in every corner selling candy, soft drinks, and newspapers. This station was deserted and silent except for the clapping from the game show on television.

The other two passengers who got off in Charlottesville picked up their small bags and walked away.

"Excuse me," I called out. The fat woman turned, the pregnant one kept walking. "How do I get to the university campus?"

"Wail," said the woman slowly, revealing a missing canine. "'S not too far if yuh wanna walk. 'S that a-way bout a mile or so. There maht be a taxi round here somewhere."

She started shuffling away, then turned and said, "Wail, come on now."

I understood almost nothing she said.

I followed her, not sure what else to do, heaving my army-green duffel bag across my back, gritting my teeth as I dragged the two suitcases, whose wheels seemed to want to roll in different directions. Outside, by the curb, were two yellow cabs. On the back of one was printed: IT'S NICE TO BE IMPORTANT, BUT IT'S IMPORTANT TO BE NICE.

I felt hysterical laughter bubbling up.

"Well, lookie here," the woman said. "Here yuh go, sugah. Two. Jus' tek yur pick. Yuh tek care now."

A driver got out of the first cab and loaded my bags. Getting in, he looked at me from the rearview mirror.

"To the University of Virginia," I said.

"Where at th' university?"

"Pardon?"

Nothing these people said made any sense. My English teacher in high school was from England. Either she taught me the wrong language or I had forgotten more English than I thought.

"Do you want to go to old dorms, new dorms, the library, to the Rotunda, where?" He spoke slightly louder and with exaggerated patience. Like he had to deal with idiotic passengers all the time.

I felt queasy. Too tired, too much bad coffee on the plane.

"I don't know where I need to go. I just need to get to the student dormitories."

"Didn't they give you an address?"

"Yes. Wait." I rubbed my gritty eyes, trying to think. I dug through my backpack and found a large manila envelope containing the welcome packet.

"Is this it?" I handed him a sheet of paper.

"Now we're getting somewhere."

We pulled away. I thought I'd feel excited by now. Nervous, edgy, alert. Instead, I just felt slow and stupid. It was hard to remember to speak in English. Everyone here seemed to speak through a mouthful of syrup.

He pulled up beside a three-story building, one of several that all looked alike. The street was nearly empty.

"Guess you're here a little early," he said. "Let me tell you, that's a good thing. This place is a zoo on moving day. You wouldn't believe what some people bring with them to college."

I couldn't think of anything to say to that. I had three bags.

I got out of the car and stood while he heaved out my suitcases from the trunk. I paid him and watched as he got into his cab. He rolled down his window.

"Good luck," he said.

I turned to face my new building, red brick with white trim on the windows and doors. Leaving my suitcases on the sidewalk, I walked up and tried the doors.

"Shit."

I rested my head on the locked doors and fought the urge to cry.

I didn't have a key.

I sat down on the steps and rummaged through my bag, opened the welcome packet, and started to read. I should have pored over this when I first got it in Israel. But at the time, I didn't have the patience to read through all the introductions and congratulations and regulations regarding personal vehicles and maximum voltage and open flames. Now I had nothing better to do. I started, hoping that at some point in this twenty-page manuscript it would tell me where to go and get a bloody key.

I was only on page five, doggedly plowing through the section about the dining facilities, opening hours, and extended meal plans, when I heard someone coming.

A woman in baggy sweats carrying a cart full of cleaning supplies walked out of one building and was headed my way.

"Hello," I said. She was the first person I'd seen since the taxi left.

"Locked out?" She seemed amused. She walked past me, eyeing the suitcases strewn around me.

"Yes. So stupid of me. I was so worried about getting here, I didn't think about the key."

"I can let you in," she said. "I've got the master key for all the rooms. Which one is yours?"

I handed her the same sheet I showed the taxi driver. I wanted to kiss her. I wanted to tell her she had no idea what this meant to me. I wanted to tell her that I just flew in from Israel, that this was only my second time ever in the United States and I wasn't sure that I liked it. But I didn't say anything.

"You're on the third floor, room 305."

I nodded.

"Follow me."

I did, grabbing my duffel bag, trusting the others would still be there when I went back for them.

She unlocked my room with a key she pulled out of her pocket.

"Make sure you go tomorrow and get a key," she said. "These rooms really need to stay locked and I don't want to get in trouble."

"You won't," I said. "I won't tell someone . . . anyone." My English was coming out badly. I wasn't sure I was saying anything right.

She waved away my promises. "Don't worry about it, just get your own key as soon as you can. It's too late to worry about it today anyhow."

My room was fairly large, but with two beds, two desks, and two closets there wasn't much room left for anything else. There were two shelves above each bed, and one window. Gray floor, white walls. Home, sweet dorm.

I dropped off my bag, tossed my backpack on the bed farthest away from the door, went back, and hauled the rest of my gear up to my room. Then I went to find the cleaning lady. She was in the bathroom, mopping the floor with brown soapy water that reeked.

"Thanks," I said. "I don't know how long I would be sitting there if it wasn't for you."

She stopped mopping and straightened.

"You're welcome."

"What's your name?"

"Yami," she said. "My name is Yami Bouchon." She sounded slightly defensive, as if she thought I was going to write down her name and file a complaint.

"I'm Maya," I said. "Maya Laor." I stuck out my hand. There was a slight hesitation on her part. We shook.

"Where are you from?" she finally asked. "Seems like you came from far away."

Now was my chance to make something up. To leave everything behind like I dreamed about when I finally decided to come. I debated inventing a life in Bulgaria with a mad uncle locked away in a castle. A fairy tale to live in. Forget where I came from. Forget what I'd done. But I heard myself tell the truth.

Back in my room, I dug around in my big suitcase until I found a sheet and a thin blanket. I'd have to buy a pillow first thing tomorrow. I left mine at home because I ran out of room in my suitcases. For now, I rolled up a sweatshirt. Lumpy, but it worked.

I thought I'd fall asleep immediately. I was tired enough to sleep until noon the next day. But I kept thinking about things; about being here, about what would happen next week when classes started. I rolled over and grabbed a notepad and made a list of all the things I had to buy tomorrow.

I heard Yami finish in the bathroom. She swept the hall, starting at the far end, working steadily. Only after the hall door clicked shut behind her did I realize I still didn't know where to get a key or whether the doors locked automatically when shut.

"Tomorrow," I said out loud. "Deal with it tomorrow." I resolutely turned over on my side, faced the wall, and willed myself to sleep.

* * *

The next morning, I woke up at six, confused with half-remembered dreams crowding my peripheral vision. On the bright side, I mostly slept through the night, waking up only twice. That alone was enough to put me in a better mood, and I hurried to get ready to explore this new place.

Once I got out of the university area, I found a Colonial-looking downtown with red-brick buildings and green-black shutters that housed everything from law offices to shops to restaurants. My favorite part was a little pedestrian-only boulevard full of small cafés and semi-expensive boutiques selling pretty nonsense. I bought breakfast at one of the coffee shops and sat down, fortified by strong coffee to plow through that damned welcome packet once and for all.

This time, not paralyzed with tiredness, I easily found the housing part and read where to get a key. The office was open from eight to five, which left me almost an hour before they opened. I studied the people huddled around mismatched tables, laughing or working in the chic café. A not-so-young mother and a blond toddler shared a muffin and a cup of hot chocolate.

My mother used to take me to coffee shops when I went with her on errands. She taught me to drink coffee. I learned to drink it to please her, to be able to share with her the joy of a really good cup of café au lait. Watching the mother and her daughter cheered me. People here couldn't be too strange if they brought their kids to cafés in the morning.

But people did look different here, I decided after a careful study of my fellow patrons and the people strolling outside the café. Clothes were baggier, hair was lighter, the colors, the styles—different. They walked differently, the pitch of conversations more relaxed, slower.

I finished my lemon-blueberry muffin, shouldered my backpack, and with one last look at the strange artwork hanging on one wall and the warped mirrors hanging on the other, I left.

It was a balmy day, not nearly as scorching as the day before. There was a slight breeze, and when I stood in the shade of the large tree on the pedestrian walk, it was actually comfortable.

"Excuse me."

I turned.

"I think this is yours." It was a student who I'd seen reading a book in a corner of the café. He was holding my welcome packet.

"Oh." I reached for it. "Thank you."

"You left it on the table." He was tall, much taller than I expected seeing him engrossed in his book. I took a small step back and saw that he noticed.

"You're a student here?" he asked.

"Going to be."

"Welcome." He spread his arms to encompass the university, Charlottesville, and the whole United States.

He looked very American to me with his light-brown hair and golden tan. I wondered if he was from some place like Nantucket or Cape Cod, places that seemed ridiculously American, like parodies of themselves. My family and I spent a couple of months in Boston once, where my father took a summer course. We traveled on the weekends when my father was free, and the small towns and the friendly people living there had seemed like scenes from a movie.

"Justin," he said, offering me his perfect hand to shake. "Justin Case. I'm working on my doctorate in history at UVA."

His name confused me at first. Said quickly it sounded like "just in case" and it took me a moment to realize that his name was first name: Justin, last name: Case.

"Right," I said, my teacher's British English stumbling on my lips. We shook. What a funny language English was. Did his parents realize his name sounded like a sentence when they named him?

"My name is Maya Laor."

"Where are you from, Maya Laor?"

"I'm from out of town."

"I noticed," he said. "From where, though? Your accent is very different."

"Greenland," I said, trying out the lie.

"You're tan," he said with a hint of a smile. "To be coming from Greenland."

"It's a beautiful country." I resisted the urge to fiddle with my packet. "Vastly underrated. We have fabulous summers."

"Really? I never knew that. The things you learn every day."

"Right."

"Nice meeting you, Maya."

"Right. Bye."

I walked away, unsure of why I was so annoyed, why my

heart raced. I thought he was watching me; but when I looked over my shoulder, he had already gone back into the café.

Walking back to the university area, I tried hard to enjoy the moment, the slow walk, the beautiful weather, the quaint shops and restaurants. When would triumph set in? When would I finally feel this success? I was going to UVA, I was out of Israel, I was going to get a college degree. I was miserable.

Tiredness lurked behind my skin, settling in my bones. It wasn't jet lag. It was the same crippling weakness from Israel. Determined to ignore it, to make it go away, I took deep breaths as I walked, rubbing a fist against my stomach to ease the tension.

After Dov died, everyone had advice. My parents wanted me to keep seeing a counselor. My aunt thought I should go to Europe for a cost-be-damned vacation—she even offered to pay for it—and then come back and focus on getting a good job. She claimed she could get me that too. My best friend, Daphna, decided I needed to learn to meditate, possibly followed by a visit to an Indian ashram. She gave me books with pictures of emaciated yogis perched on the edge of a cliff, as if they were teaching the miracles of human flight instead of meditation. But it was nothing any books could help with. We both knew that.

Nobody thought I should leave for four years. Six months, twelve months, that was fine. Everyone went traveling after the army. But four years? That's a long time to be gone. To run away. They were right, of course. That was the point.

I bought everything on my list. Got a key to the room. Tried to stay busy. The next day, I bought all the books I needed for my classes. They were obscenely expensive and I used the credit card my parents gave me, feeling guilty. The books for my two astronomy classes were beautiful, though. I spent almost an hour sitting on a bench in an enclosed garden behind one of the pavilions on the Lawn, looking at the pictures. The garden itself was something of a pleasant surprise. Like everyone who visited the university, I strolled by the Rotunda, admiring its perfect lines. Trying to see the backs of the pavilions that stretch out from it, I discovered that each pavilion had a garden open to the public. Each garden was different, perfect and beautiful in its own way. I tested out several before picking a favorite, the one behind Pavilion IV. Some of the gardens were open and seemed designed for parties or picnics, but Garden IV seemed designed for quiet thought. There were more lush bushes and full trees, more green and fewer flowers. The pavilion was almost hidden from sight, and sitting on the white bench tucked up against the red-brick fence, I could pretend I was happy to be here.

I found the library and used the Internet to write to my friends Daphna, Leah, and Irit, and my brother Adam. Leah had just been to a show by a modern-dance troupe I'd been wanting to see. Daphna wrote me a message complaining about her job, like always. I wished I were still there so I could take her out for a cup of coffee and we could both vent about stupid co-workers. I e-mailed my parents as well, letting them know how I was, how my room looked, that I was doing great, brilliant, everyone here so nice.

I spent three days almost completely alone. I spoke only when ordering breakfast or lunch at the café or when I bought something at a store. I saw Yami twice, and we waved to each other but didn't speak. I slept a lot, flipped through my books, and walked for hours, exploring the university and the town.

It was exactly four months since the funeral. Not even half a year. I knew my parents didn't want me to think about it. But it wasn't right not to think of it, of him. A person should linger with you after he dies. Besides, trying not to think of him was an exercise in futility.

On the fourth day after I arrived, the rest of the students came.

I woke up at seven to the sounds of shouted directions.

"No, Mom, not there! Here, here it is."

Within two hours, the halls were jammed and the flow of new students seemed like it would never end.

It was hard to believe that this was the same street from five days ago. Cars were parked up on the curb, stopped in the middle of the road, hazard lights flashing. Hundreds of people were carrying brown boxes, straining, laughing that nervous laugh of stress and exertion. People were shouting to be careful, to lift on THREE, to please move your car so we can get through. Older students in blue shirts were helping new students move in. Parents were hugging their embarrassed children, kissing their foreheads, looking on fondly and with concerned pride as they helped them unpack their favorite shirts and their lucky shoes. The students seemed so young, with round faces and shining eyes. Only two years younger than I was, but they seemed infantile.

Every door was propped open. People were meeting their hallmates, assessing the people they would have to live with for the next year. Some were scratching their heads at the logistics of cramming a TV and a mini-fridge into a room already stuffed. Closets bulged, beds were elevated on cement blocks to make storage space. Minivans and station wagons careened out to make last-minute purchases of shelves, rugs, and cinder blocks. It was chaos.

At first I thought I'd stick around and meet my new roommate, but as the halls got more and more crowded, I decided we would have plenty of time to get to know each other. I slipped out and headed to the Corner, the area near the university that seemed to cater to the student population, thinking to buy a cup of coffee. It was disorienting to have so many people around after pure silence. But even away from the dorms it was a mad rush of buying supplies and greeting old friends and introducing new acquaintances on the narrow cobbled sidewalk. Students buying books, buying T-shirts with VIRGINIA emblazoned across the front, reiterating their triumph of arriving here.

I turned and walked away from there as well. Crowds made me nervous, even well-behaved American crowds. The town felt flooded with people. There were suddenly minor traffic jams at every light. There were no parking spaces. The stores were full, cash registers dinging in joy. I really didn't care about meeting people, learning their names. They all seemed so young. They all looked alike. They dressed the same. The guys with their hats pulled low, slouching in their khaki shorts and gray T-shirts while the girls all wore cute little outfits that I hadn't seen since I was a kid—baby-doll shirts, flowery skirts, high-heeled sandals or colored canvas shoes. Their blondish hair was pulled high up in cheerful ponytails.

Wearing dark-blue jeans and a black tank top, I felt old compared with them, like a big, dark lizard in the baby-animal petting zoo.

As the day wore on, parents began to retreat, to start their long drives home, to leave their kids alone and let them settle in. I decided it was safe to return and entered my building, which was nearly humming with chatter and nervous energy.

The door to my room was open, and four half-full suitcases lay on the floor. I peered in.

"Hello?" I said.

A girl turned from the closet, her arms full of folded shirts.

"Hi!" she said brightly.

"I'm your roommate," I said. "My name is Maya Laor."

"Oh, hi!" she said again, eyes wide with excitement. "I was wondering when I'd see you. I saw all your stuff already here, but I didn't know where you were."

"I got here four days ago. I hope you don't mind I took the bed by the wall."

"Oh, it doesn't matter," she said. "My name is Payton Lee Walker, most people either call me Payton or Pay."

She was short, barely reaching my chin. She had blond hair up in a ponytail and wore khaki shorts, a white T-shirt, and pink flip-flops. She fit. I wondered how she knew to wear what everyone else was wearing. Maybe it was in the welcome packet. Maybe it was an American thing.

"This is so great. You don't know how long I've waited to meet you!"

I smiled.

"I mean, it's so important who your roommate is, you know? You hear such awful stories sometimes, but I just know we'll get along great. It'll be so cool. I'm just going to finish putting some of these clothes away and then my parents want to take us out to dinner."

"You don't have to do that."

"Don't be silly. They want to get to know you, plus we live really close by. Only twenty, well, I guess closer to thirty minutes away, so it's no trouble at all. I think it's hard on them that I'm leaving. I'm the baby of the family. Two older brothers." She rolled her eyes. "At least I'm going to UVA, my brothers both got as far away from here as they could." She laughed.

I nodded, hardly able to keep up with her chatter.

"How about you? How are your parents taking this?"

"They're fine," I said. "They're used to me not living at home. But they didn't expect for me to go so far away."

"Where do you live?"

"Haifa, in Israel."

"Jeez, that's really far away. I don't think your packet says you're an international student."

Didn't she notice my accent? Did she think it was polite to ignore it?

"International students are supposed to live in a different dorm, I think. With other international students, but I'm glad you're here."

I was silent, not sure what to say.

"Much more interesting, I think. It's cool you're from Israel. Is it really dangerous there? I always hear about it on the news."

I was quiet.

She hesitated for a moment, finally hearing the words that gushed out. She turned back to her closet and straightened a row of folded shirts. "I think it's great," she said firmly as if I had contradicted her. "My parents are excited to meet you."

I wasn't sure about that.

She was like a puppy. Jumping from topic to topic, flitting around the room, cramming her clothes into already-packed shelves, hanging dress after dress, glancing back at me every so often to make sure I was still there.

"Daddy!" she said when a paunchy, silver-haired man stood at our door. "This is Maya, my new roommate."

"Hey, honey." He kissed her on the forehead. "I see you've been busy while I was gone."

Payton smiled. The room looked like her closet had exploded. She was developing a "system," she had explained, and wanted each article of clothing in its proper spot.

"It's nice to meet you, Maya," Payton's father said,

extending a hand. We shook, my hand nearly swallowed up in his. "Payton's been looking forward to meeting you all summer."

He had a nice voice, slow and deep. And an accent mild enough that I understood most of what he said.

"Me too," I said. I hadn't given half a thought to my roommate or who she was. "It's nice to finally meet her, and you." I bit my lip.

"My wife and I were hoping you will join us for dinner."

"I don't know—"

"Come on, Maya," Payton said. "Just come."

"Thank you," I said. I didn't have anything else to do and the dorm would be packed and impossible to get away from. "That's very nice of you."

"Nonsense. Come on, girls, Payton's mom is in the car waiting for us."

Payton's parents were well bred, well mannered, and well off. Exactly what I expected. Her father ("Robert, but please call me Bob") was a lawyer, working at the same firm his father worked at, his grandfather had worked at, and his great-grandfather had founded. Her mother (who told me to call her Sissy, but didn't really seem to mean it) was extremely busy with something called the Junya League, the Republican Party, and their church. Of Payton's two brothers, one attended Stanford, then UVA law school, and was now cutting his teeth at the firm's Richmond office. Her oldest brother, a bit of a nonconformist, went to the University of Chicago ("A Yankee school in a Yankee city," to his parents' horror), was an investment banker, and currently lived in Hong Kong with his Chinese girlfriend ("lovely girl, very sweet").

We spoke about Charlottesville—they told me funny stories about ghosts in the hallways and a cow that had been lifted on top of the Rotunda, a practical joke at the turn of the century.

"Charlottesville and the university in particular are just lovely areas," Payton's mother said. "But you shouldn't forget that it can be dangerous. Especially for girls like you."

She must have seen the disbelief that crossed my face.

"I know it looks calm and staid, but last year two students were brutally beaten. They were in the hospital for weeks." She leaned in. "The police never caught the man who did it. They said it was a fraternity hazing gone wrong, but I don't believe that for a second. Whoever did it is still out there."

I made a suitably concerned face. These people might as well have been from Mars.

"Now, Sissy, don't go giving the girl nightmares."

I tried to imagine what kind of person would develop nightmares from a story like that. I just couldn't picture it.

"I just think you need to be aware," she said carefully. "Both of you. Try to stick together."

That evening, as Payton and I settled in for our first night together, Payton sighed and stretched.

"I think this year is going to be great," she said. "I was really scared before I came here, but now I'm finally getting excited about all this." She stretched and sighed. "Yeah, this year is going to be great."

I smiled at her in the dark but didn't say anything.

I didn't think this year could be any worse than the last, but you never knew for sure, did you?

Chapter Two

ISRAEL

My high school buddies and I were at our favorite hangout, a café and bar on the beach. Our usual table on the deck was full of our empty glasses and wet napkins. It was only a few weeks before we were scheduled to begin basic training. We tried to be cool and nonchalant, legs sprawled, arms casually folded.

"You know, it's up to us now," Alon said. "We're the great Israeli hope. Saddam and Arafat won't know what hit them once we sign up."

We all laughed loudly.

"Yeah, they'll be like, why is that tank pointing the wrong way, right?" Daphna said.

"Oh yeah," David said. "Heck, yeah. They'll be like—why is that redheaded soldier holding his rifle upside down?" He high-fived Alon, who was infamous at the arcade for shooting aliens, robbers, and vampires holding his gun upside down.

We whooped and cheered. We clinked our Diet Cokes.

Life was good. I was excited.

The day I packed for boot camp, my brother Adam leaned against the doorframe of my bedroom and watched me for a while.

"I still can't believe you're going," he said, shaking his head.

"I know." I flashed him a quick grin.

"Are you nervous?"

"Naw."

"Bullshit."

I laughed. "All right, then," I said. "I guess you know best."

"I can't wait to go," he said fiercely. At fifteen, he hadn't hit his growth spurt. It bothered him, made him feel he had to prove how tough he was.

"Your time will come," I said. "Everyone goes." I sat back on my heels, looking at the piles of T-shirts, shorts, and socks around me. "And you'll give Mom a heart attack and Dad an ulcer by volunteering for some crazy combat unit."

He grinned at me and looked so young I felt my heart squeeze.

"I'm going to miss you," I said.

"Yeah, Maya, me too." His voice was a bit husky, a hint of things to come. "Don't be scared. You'll be okay."

I stopped and looked at him. His hair was gelled in spikes and he was wearing baggy jeans and high-top sneakers scribbled with Magic Marker. Skater cool.

"Thanks, Adam," I said quietly.

"Any time." Then a look crossed his face that I knew so well.

"What? What evil thought did you just have?"

He had that smug tilt to his smile.

"What?" I asked again.

"Well, I was just going to say I hope you become a bad-ass soldier. . . ."

"Yeah?"

"Not a big-ass soldier."

It was common knowledge that many girls gained weight during their military service. They'd fill out their assigned uniforms until the seams stretched near bursting. I threw my pillow at him and missed. It went sailing over his shoulder. He laughed at me and ran out, suddenly a kid again.

That night, my mother cooked my favorite meal, noodles with meat sauce. Kipi, our dog, sat near me and I slipped her the big chunks of meat from my sauce. My parents disliked it when I fed her at the table, but this time they pretended not to notice. They kept looking at me and sighing.

"Come on, guys," I said. "You're making me crazy."

"Yeah," Adam said. "It's not like she's going to a combat unit. They'll probably have her answering phones in a week."

I leaned over to smack him on the back of the head.

"You're going to be a secretary," he taunted, leaping back from his seat as I lunged after him. "Maya's a secretary, Maya's a secretary," he sang.

I took off and chased him around the apartment. Kipi ran after us, barking and jumping to nip my heels.

Before I went to sleep that night, my parents came to my room to say good night.

"I can't believe you won't be here tomorrow night," my mother said. "My little *pashoshi*, my baby chick is all grown up."

"You're going to have a great time," my father said. "Some things will be really awful, like the food. But you'll make great friends and you'll grow up."

I had heard this speech before.

"The military is a great experience," he continued. "It teaches you about discipline and order. Focus. Teamwork."

"*Abba*, I know. You've told me."

"Have I?" he asked. "Well that's good advice I gave you."

"I'll be fine."

"Of course you will," my mother said briskly. "Look at us here, acting like something awful's about to happen. Maya, you'll do great, you'll have fun. I had a great time during my basic training. I'll have you know I was a crack shot."

I burst out laughing.

"What? What's funny about that?"

"Oh, *Ima*," I said, snorting. "A crack shot?"

My mother was round, like an apple, and would shriek like a car alarm at the sight of a cockroach.

"That's right," she said with dignity. "I always hit my mark."

"*Leila tov*," my father said. "Good night."

"Good night," I called out. I could hear my mother protesting as they walked away. "What's so funny about being a crack shot? You know I was."

I lay in bed that night, memorizing my room, wondering how much I might miss it. I couldn't stop thinking about how I'd look wearing a uniform. Some girls looked so awful in them, and there was nothing you could do about it.

I went over my packing list again, trying to think if I forgot anything. My mom and I had gone out and bought several packages of white T-shirts and white socks, and I could only wear brown or black hair bands and barrettes. I packed workout clothes, running shoes, shampoo and conditioner, a hairbrush, nail clippers, tampons, but there was that nagging feeling that maybe I'd forgotten something and I'd be stuck without it. I didn't sleep well that night. I kept waking up, thinking it was morning already.

In the morning my mom drove me to the central pickup point for Haifa, where all the girls leaving for boot camp assembled. With so many families seeing their girls off, it was hard to get to where I needed to go. At first I wasn't even sure where I was supposed to be; it almost felt like a party. Parents took pictures, kissed and hugged, and tucked in extra sandwiches for their girls to eat or to share. I looked at my mom and she smiled and hugged me.

The buses drove us to Tel Hashomer, where everyone started out on the first day of their military service. Buses with girls from all the other pick-up centers kept arriving, one after another. It was amazing the number of girls, like me, milling around, chatting, trying to look like they knew what was happening, but failing. After we got off the bus, there were soldiers with clipboards, reading names off a list. Within an hour, we were separated into squads and formed the "soldier necklace." We followed one another, like beads strung on a necklace, each picking up an empty kit bag and then walking from station to station, collecting equipment. You entered the necklace a civilian and you left it a soldier.

I signed for two types of uniforms: training and formal; two belts: one for each type of uniform; sandals, skirt, hat, a first-aid kit, and dog tags with my name and personal number. When I finished with my service, I'd have to return most of the stuff.

I rolled up my sleeve and a nurse with a gunlike injector shot a triple cocktail of vaccines into the meat of my left shoulder.

After everyone was done with the necklace, we assembled in squads and stood at attention.

"Heads up!" a drill sergeant shouted the first time we stood in formation. "Shoulders back!" My chin practically pointed at the sky. I was arched back so far I felt like I might fall over. It seemed a bit silly, standing there in my new uniform, my shoulder blades nearly touching.

The drill sergeant inspected each girl, tugging at uniforms, nudging chins. When she had us arranged to her liking, she stood in front of us, her legs shoulder-width apart, elbows bent, hands behind her back.

"Welcome to boot camp," she said coldly. "Don't expect a vacation. You will work hard and study hard. I expect you to pass your classes and your physical training. Failure to follow orders will result in unpleasant consequences." She stressed the word unpleasant. "If you follow orders, if you are disciplined, if you are not lazy, fat, or slovenly, then I think we will get along fine. If you are spoiled, if you are lazy, if you are disobedient, then I think"—she paused for a second, then smiled—"then I think we will have a very interesting three weeks."

We were herded onto buses again. These drove us to where the actual boot-camp training took place. I wasn't the only one who hadn't slept the night before. As soon as the bus pulled away and that humming purr of the engine settled into its highway lullaby, I saw heads nod forward or tilt at odd angles as nearly everyone fell asleep.

I woke up when the bus lurched to a stop and the girl sitting next to me grabbed my hand.

"We're here," she said.

Once we got off the bus, the twelve of us in my squad huddled together until the instructor we were assigned to found us. The boot-camp instructors, Makits, were aloof and took themselves very seriously. Like the rest of the Makits, ours wore the brim of her hat pulled low over her eyes. She stood in front of us when she had us line up and I hated that I couldn't tell where she was looking. She showed us our barracks. We dropped off our gear on the narrow beds and then fell in again outside.

"My name is Drill Sergeant Orit," she said. She sounded much calmer than the drill sergeant at Tel Hashomer. "There are three basic sections to your training: weapons training, chemical and biological weapons protection, and first aid. Every day, wake-up is at five. You have thirty minutes before morning formation. After formation, you'll participate in morning physical training, then morning inspection. After that, you go to the dining hall for breakfast." She outlined the standard schedule of each day.

I liked knowing when and where I was supposed to be. The program sounded tedious but not terribly hard. I can do this, I thought. This isn't such a big deal. Our Makit seemed very sensible, and she explained things clearly and simply. Just when I was ready to write off Drill Sergeant Orit as a good egg, one of the girls in the squad blew a bubble-gum bubble and it popped loudly. Orit stalked over to the girl.

"What do you think you're doing?"

The girl looked a bit surprised. "I'm chewing gum. What, aren't we allowed to chew gum?"

"Soldier!" Orit barked, startling us all. "You do not have permission to look me in the eye!"

All of us sucked in our breath and, while looking straight ahead, tried to see what was going on.

"You are not allowed to chew gum! You are not allowed to blow bubbles! And you are not allowed to be disrespectful!"

I think what shocked me the most was how quickly Orit went from being a reasonable-sounding person to this snarling beast. I made a note to step lightly around her.

That night, the girl from the bunk above mine stood by the bed, trying to look over her shoulder at her butt. She kept twisting and craning her neck. A lot of the girls were pretty miserable about their uniforms. Even the smallest amount of belly fat looked like a jelly roll in the ill-fitting khaki-green shirt. People's butts never looked right in the uniform either.

"It's not as bad as you think," I told her.

She snorted. "Do you think they designed them to make us look fat on purpose?"

"Probably," I said. I remembered her from the bus ride. Irit was hard to miss, being half a head taller than everyone else. Leah, in the bunk next to mine, was her cousin.

"I hope to God we have a better Makit than my sister did two years ago," Irit said, sitting down on my bed. "You wouldn't believe some of the stuff she put that squad through."

I sat cross-legged at the foot of my bed, and Leah sat on hers, leaning against the wall.

"I don't think ours will be like that," Leah said. "She seemed pretty nice, actually."

"Were you standing in formation with the rest of us?" I asked.

Leah shrugged. "That's just to set the mood. You can't take these things too seriously."

"Don't take it seriously, huh?" Irit snorted. "Let's see you not take it seriously when she has us run the base perimeter for the fifteenth time."

"That'll just get us fit and skinny," Leah said.

Irit stared at her for a moment, not sure if she was serious. Leah started laughing. Pretty soon all three of us were laughing, the kind of laugh where you don't even know why you're laughing, but everything keeps cracking you up.

A few minutes later, the lights went out. I lay in my narrow cot on the rough cotton sheets, surrounded by the soft sounds of a dozen girls settling down for bed. I quickly fell asleep, utterly drained by the long day.

* * *

I soon discovered that boot camp was like summer camp without a swimming pool, field trips, or arts and crafts. We were on our feet a lot, learning to march from here to there. We learned all about the Uzi and the M-16: how to assemble them, how to clean them, how to fire them. I was surprised how much I enjoyed the satisfying clicks that cool black metal made as it slid and locked into place. Each night, we dropped our disassembled firearms in a vat of oil. The next morning, we had to clean all the parts until not a drop of oil or a speck of dirt remained.

At inspection, we stood at attention next to our beds, our weapons in pieces on them. Orit stood by the door and called us to attention when Lieutenant Meirav entered our barracks. I worked hard that morning to clean my weapon, and it certainly looked clean lying on my bed. There were certain parts, though, that no matter how much you cleaned them, you couldn't get all the oil out. Meirav, in charge of weapons inspection, knew that, of course. She picked up each piece and examined it from every side.

"I'm looking for elephants," she said the first time she did it.

I smiled, not sure if sarcasm meant she wanted me to answer or not.

Just when I thought she was done and I'd passed inspection, she picked up the one piece I hadn't managed to get perfectly clean. She stuck her pinkie in it and then held it in front of my face so I could see the oily smear on her finger.

"What's this?" Meirav asked. It was obvious what it was, so

I didn't answer. There was nothing I could say. My stomach growled. We'd been up for two hours and hadn't had breakfast yet.

"Your weapon," she said, inches from my face, "will keep you alive. It will keep your fellow soldiers alive. Show it some respect, Private Maya, or it will fail you when you need it most."

That was a big joke, of course, because the weapons they gave us to practice with were ancient. Irit joked that she recognized hers from a textbook photo of weapons used in the 1940s during the War of Independence. No one really thought we would ever use them to stay alive. I knew what Meirav was saying was just a pose, and she knew I knew. But I also knew what she meant. In the end, a weapon was a thing that was designed to hurt, to kill, and it demanded respect.

Few inspections went by when she didn't pick my weapon to inspect. Sometimes I wondered if Orit told her to pick on me, because she only inspected three or four weapons each time, so it was sheer perversity that made her constantly choose mine.

Lieutenant Meirav nearly always found a trace of oil in a tiny crevice that I had somehow missed. For a brief second, her face would light up in a cold smile. She hid it in a frown of disgust and disappointment, but I knew she was glad that she'd found something wrong.

Each time I failed inspection, my stomach dropped and my afternoon would be shot, wasted on re-cleaning and extra duty for failing to clean the weapon well enough in the first place.

Twice, though, I did it perfectly. Meirav wanted to find something wrong, but she looked and looked and finally walked away without saying a word. I couldn't stop grinning for half an hour.

When we weren't on the field, we were in the classroom learning about enemy positions, equipment, strengths and weaknesses. In military strategy we memorized battle plans of past wars. Not particularly grueling; not particularly interesting either.

I had a harder time with the firing range. I both loved it and dreaded it, and unlike my mother, I was not a crack shot. On the one hand, it was oh so cool to be lying in the dirt, eyes squinting at the man-shaped target. It fit with the image I had of myself as a tough soldier . . . a deadly, dangerous woman to be reckoned with. On the other hand, it was scary because there were no dividers between each shooter and I always worried that the girl lying next to me would lose control of her weapon, have it skid sideways, and accidentally shoot me. Perhaps my habit of keeping an eye on the shooter on either side of me kept me from hitting my target as often as I would have liked. One eye to the left and one to the right didn't really leave you with much to look straight ahead.

Each time, the range Makit would shout the command to drop down to shooting position. We'd all drop down to the dirt lying on our stomachs, one arm extended along the length of the barrel, gripping the handle, the other curled around the trigger. I'd wait until I heard "Cock your weapon. Aim." I'd close my left eye, sighting down the length of the barrel, the target fuzzy in the distance. My heart would start beating faster. Then the range instructor would call out, "The targets are before you, fire at will." I shot quickly and sloppily, my target speckled with the occasional hit, my ears ringing from the noise. We were given earplugs, but they only muffled the sound.

It was always dusty, and I was usually sweaty and grimy. But I never looked forward to the showers because they had no curtains. At first I tried to figure out some way to shower without anyone seeing anything, but that was impossible. It took me a while before I could strip and shower without feeling my skin crawling with invisible eyes. But after a while, the sight of a bunch of naked, soapy butts stopped bothering me and I just didn't care who saw my boobs. I probably stopped caring because I was so tired. By law, we were required to get six hours of sleep a night. Our Makit made sure that's about all we got.

In boot camp they wanted me to overcome the overwhelming urge to hide, duck, take cover, and disappear. Instead, I was taught to stand up, take action, grab a rifle, and shoot. Our basic training took place in a mini-base inside the perimeter of a "real" base. We had our own perimeter to patrol and our own "safety hole" where bombs could be detonated.

On my first few patrol duties, I was fully alert, my eyes and ears twitchy to every movement around me. I felt personally responsible for keeping the rest of my bunkmates safe. Irit waited three days before pointing out that the guys get to patrol the outer perimeter of the real base and that everything we were doing was just pretend. That took away a lot of the excitement of guard duty. After that I really didn't take it seriously.

Once the thrill was gone, I tried to laugh at our Makit's seriousness, her melodramatic insistence on aggressive perfection. I felt foolish for ever believing this was serious business. I tried to maintain the mocking pose I was so famous for in high school.

"These people need to remove the sticks from their asses. It's not as if we'll ever see combat," I grumbled to Leah. Quiet and easygoing, her pale skin full of ginger-colored freckles, she never got boiling mad the way Irit and I did.

She shrugged, her moon-face unusually serious.

"You never know," she said.

That's the thing about Leah. She was quiet, but she had a way with words. I shut up and stopped complaining . . . at least about that.

When the three weeks of boot camp were finally over, we had a "breaking of the distance" and all the instructors who had been distant and aloof came over and gave us big hugs and said we were a great group, one of the best they'd ever taught. Irit rolled her eyes at Leah and me, but I just smiled. It turned out that our Makit, who'd been training us, punishing us, and occasionally praising us for the past three weeks, who was so commanding and stern, was only three months older than me. I'd been sure she was at least two years older.

The same day, most people received their assignments. I'd already been told the week before that I'd be sent to a one-week administrator course. What mattered was the assignment after that. On impulse, I requested a posting "away from home." My parents lived in Haifa, but I was hoping to get posted near Tel Aviv. My aunt lived in the heart of the city and it would be fun to live there with her. There was always a lot going on in Tel Aviv, and between concerts and comedy shows and funky shops, you could count on finding something fun to do on the weekend.

Both Leah and Irit had requested to be stationed near their homes. With her high scores, Leah was assigned to a military-intelligence course. Irit, like me, got the administrator's course.

One of the girls from our squad had a camera and she took our picture, right at the end.

I loved the picture, the three of us slim like Leah predicted, and tanned, arms draped over one another, looking very comfortable in our khaki uniforms.

Six of us from our barracks received a week's leave, and Irit invited us to her parents' house on the banks of the Kineret.

Irit put on MTV's greatest hits, and the whole room throbbed with the bass from the speakers mounted on the walls. In the kitchen Leah made mystery punch. I was well into my third drink when someone bumped into me and the bright-red punch sloshed out of my cup. I watched, fascinated, as it arched out, hung suspended for a moment, and then came splashing down on the white marble floor.

I started laughing, which got Leah's attention. She looked so funny like this, loose-limbed and graceless. She tripped over a kitchen chair trying to get a closer look. Irit tried to help as

Leah fought to right herself, but she was laughing so hard that Leah fell twice more, completely tangled in the chair legs.

"I'm gonna pee in my pants," Irit shrieked while poor Leah, struggling to right herself like a bug on its back, tried to stand.

I helped Leah up and Irit leaned against the kitchen counter, gasping for breath, trying to stop the occasional giggle that kept escaping.

"Wait," she gasped. "Wait a second. We should mop this up."

Leah and I studied the red stain.

"How about a towel?"

"It'll get dirty." Irit frowned.

That seemed profound.

"I know!" Leah raced to the bathroom and came back with an armload of toilet paper.

"Perfect!"

Leah carefully laid the paper out until it covered the red puddle. Soon there was a pile of pink soggy paper in the middle of the floor.

"It looks like the kitchen had its period," Irit snorted. "Does this mean it can get pregnant?" That sent us into gales of laughter.

"Safe sex for the refrigerator!" A sudden image of humping freezers had me laughing so hard I had tears in my eyes.

Later that night, when the music stopped, the three of us stretched out on the balcony looking at the stars, and I closed my eyes and felt the world spinning under me. I could picture myself, a tiny speck on top of the perfect sphere of the earth, spinning at supersonic speed while orbiting around the sun.

"This is the start of something," Leah said. "Our real lives are starting now. What we do will finally make a difference."

"Please," Irit said. "We're just privates. We won't be doing anything important."

"That's not true. We're a part of something important."

"I'm going to be important," I said dreamily. "I'm going to have adventures. We'll have them together. I can't wait to start."

"Yeah," said Leah softly. "Me too."

We finally fell asleep on the Persian rug in the living room, and someone threw up in a potted lemon tree on the balcony. I woke up the next day with a splitting headache, compliments of my first hangover. When Irit's parents, who had barricaded themselves in their bedroom, came into the kitchen for breakfast, they were horrified. Empty bottles and half-eaten food littered their elegant flat. We never did mop up the punch from the floor, and the soggy toilet paper had started to dry on the white marble floor, staining it pink.

It was the shouting that woke me. Irit's parents yelling at her, at us, for the disaster we'd made. Irit, pale and slightly green, just stood there before them, stony-faced. She wouldn't look at them or at us.

We all gathered our stuff quietly, mumbled apologies to her parents, and left.

After the party, I came home and spent the rest of the week with my parents. I hadn't told them yet about asking to be assigned away from home. With Irit's parents' yells still ringing in my ears, I dreaded telling my parents anything that might set them off. What was I thinking, I thought with self-disgust. Why in the world had I put "away from home"? My mom would be so upset. We'd never discussed it, but I knew she assumed I'd be living at home.

I took the bus from the Kineret to Haifa, and when I descended from the bus, my parents and Adam were waiting for me.

"Look at you," Adam said, grinning from ear to ear. "You actually look like a soldier."

"Just wait until I have my very own Uzi, then I'll be a real soldier." Except that I probably wouldn't get one. Girls only got their own weapons if they were stationed at a dangerous base—like near the West Bank or Gaza, or near the border with Lebanon or Syria—or if they were combat instructors. It was always the guys that got the good weapons, a Galil or a short M-16. Girls always got the brooms, the huge rickety old M-16s that weighed a ton. I wouldn't even really want a weapon assigned, because if you had one, then you had to carry it with you whenever you were in uniform. I wondered where you put it when you went to the bathroom. Were you supposed to lay it next to you when you went to sleep?

My mother hugged me and I sank into her softness and breathed in the smell of her perfume in the crook of her neck.

"How did it go?" my father asked. He grabbed my green duffel bag and heaved it over one shoulder as we all walked to the car.

"Just like you said," I told him. I settled into the backseat of the car. "But you know, it's good to be home."

"Of course it is," he said. He put the key in the ignition. "That's why you're doing this."

I smiled at my family and felt a little more at ease. I settled into my seat with a sigh.

My mother noticed the weight loss.

"*Elohim*, dear lord," she said when we got home and she got a good look at me. "Didn't they feed you at boot camp?"

"They did," I said. "But not well."

That night, we sat down to supper, and my parents told stories about their boot-camp days. Everyone went through this in Israel; even my grandmother had served in the War of Independence, though the thought of her with a rifle in hand was absurd. I pictured her wearing high heels and an evening dress, stepping gingerly between coils of barbed wire, gritting her teeth in distress when her dress snagged. She probably argued with the platoon leader when he told her she shouldn't wear her diamonds.

Sitting in our white kitchen with the pots and pans hanging from the wall, I found out certain things never change. The sergeant was always awful, sadistic, and stupid, clearly bent on torturing the poor innocents in her care. I laughed so hard at their stories I couldn't breathe. To my amazement, I also had stories to tell that made them laugh. Already the tedium of it, the frustration, was fading. Adam gazed at me wistfully.

"I can't wait to be eighteen," he said. "It's going to be awesome."

That night, back in my narrow bed, I stretched under the covers and grinned. I agreed with Adam. Eighteen wasn't so bad at all.

The next morning, I stumbled into the living room, stifling a yawn. My mother, holding a dishtowel and a dripping bowl, stood in front of the television.

"A suicide bomber," she said, shaking her head. "Number Nine bus in Jerusalem."

The camera showed the Red Star of David crew running with stretchers and the police shouting for people to step back.

"How many dead?" I rubbed sleep from the corner of my eye. Kipi walked by. I picked her up and stroked the top of her head. She squirmed to get down.

"They're not sure yet. Twelve, maybe more."

I winced. That was a bad one. I let Kipi down and she scampered away.

"The bus was packed, kids going to school, people going to work," my mom said.

I glanced at the clock on the wall. The bomb had gone off fifteen minutes earlier, at the height of the morning rush.

We watched the news together for a while, but there was nothing more the anchor could say and the clips were repeating. The suicide bomber was dead, the bus was a blackened shell, its top popped up like a sardine can's.

"Come on, honey." My mother rose from the couch but left the television on. "Let's get you some breakfast."

"I want a cheese omelet and salad." My favorite breakfast.

I tried to shake off the uneasy feeling I had from watching the news. What a great way to start your day. You kiss your kids good-bye, send them to school, and ten minutes later your world blows apart. Every time I heard about a bombing I tried to think who I knew living in the area. Even if I hadn't thought about her in months, I'd suddenly remember that a kid I hadn't seen since junior high lived in that part of town. I could almost count on the fact that someone I knew would know someone who was hurt or killed in the blast. A friend's cousin, a neighbor's former high school teacher. The country was too small. You always knew someone who knew someone.

Irit called me later that day. In an unusually subdued voice, she told me how furious her parents were.

"They saved most of the yelling until everyone left. I don't think I ever saw them so pissed off."

"Oh, honey," I said. "That must have been awful."

"Yeah, no more parties at my place, okay?"

I called Leah after we hung up.

"I don't blame them," she said. "We were out of control, it wasn't right."

"What do you mean?" I protested. "We just got out of boot camp, we're allowed to let off some steam. It's practically a requirement."

"It was wrong, Maya, and you know it."

"No one was hurt," I grumbled.

"Irit's parents were, and I bet Irit is sorry now too."

We ended up agreeing to send Irit's parents a bouquet of sunflowers with an apology for the party.

I still hadn't told my parents about living away from home. But knowing that Leah would disapprove of that too, and since I needed to report for my course in six days, I decided to take responsibility for my actions. I told my mom. She already knew I hadn't gotten the type of job I'd wanted. I'd called nearly in tears when I first found out they were sending me to an administrator's course (basically, how to be a secretary), but now I told her I'd asked for a faraway assignment.

"Yeah," I said, and tried not to fidget. "Do you mind terribly? I just wanted to give it a try."

"Maybe you'll get Rishon Lezion," she said, naming a large base outside Tel Aviv. "That way you could live with Aunt Hen."

It was exactly what I'd been thinking when I signed up. I looked at her in surprise. She smiled.

"I think it'll be great," she said. She could tell I was amazed by her easy acceptance and it amused her. "Hen knows a lot of people," she said. "Maybe she can help out."

Two days later, Hen came to visit.

It was a hot and blindingly bright Friday afternoon. My parents and I were sitting on our balcony in the shade, sipping ice water with lemon and mint. The sky was eggshell blue, and from our fourth-story apartment I could make out the Mediterranean in the distance. I had to keep my eyes half-shut because I'd left my sunglasses at Irit's house. There was so much light in the air that it was nearly painful.

Aunt Hen came and joined us from inside.

"Oh, Michalle, what a sweet little place, it's so adorable, like a doll's house."

My mother smiled. We'd lived in this apartment for almost two years, but Hen always said that when she visited. Hen settled down, careful of her linen trousers, and sipped her drink.

If my mother was built like an apple, then Aunt Hen was an asparagus stalk, long and lean. There was only a slight family resemblance in their forehead and nose. Otherwise they looked completely different. Hen turned her green eyes on me.

"So you think you can make do in my little place?" Her place in Tel Aviv was huge. Until this new apartment, Hen, who lived alone, had a bigger place than us.

"Do you really think you can get me assigned there?" I'd called her two days ago to drop the bomb.

"It's a large base, they always need people." Aunt Hen gave her little cat smile, which I took to be a positive sign.

Hen was my mother's younger sister and she'd never married, although knowing Hen, it was probably by choice. I wondered if my parents minded her dig at their place. My mother seemed to have made peace with her sister long ago. I never saw her upset by any of the sharp cracks Aunt Hen tossed out as casually as breathing. My father was frequently annoyed by her and often stayed away when she came to visit. Part of the problem was that Hen believed Haifa, despite being the third-largest city in Israel, was a backwater province. Only Tel Aviv existed on her map of success. She'd criticized my father in the past for not opening an office there.

"It'll be fun having you with me," she finally said to me. "I can take you to all my parties and you can meet cabinet ministers and actors and journalists." She gave a little laugh. "I can't wait to show you around. Maybe you'll even meet someone and thank me at your wedding."

My father shifted in annoyance and my mother glanced his way.

"Maya's a little young to be dating politicians," he said.

"I didn't say anything about dating politicians. But let's face it, Yakov, no matter what Maya decides to do after getting out, knowing the right people won't hurt." She nudged me with her toe and I smiled. "You'll love Tel Aviv, Maya, it's where everything happens."

Chapter Three

VIRGINIA

In my eagerness to leave Israel, I had brushed aside the difficulties of thinking and living in another language. By the time evening came around, my brain would cry out to stop thinking in English. It would short-circuit in Hebrew and I would stand there, gaping like a fish out of water, struggling to find that elusive slippery English word.

I spoke with my parents almost every morning. I could feel Payton looking at me curiously as I chatted with them in Hebrew on the phone. My parents wanted to know about everything—the food, the weather, Payton, my professors. I spent hours talking to them. I always felt a little hollow by the time I got off the phone, as if I'd just emptied out all the experiences of the day, leaving me with nothing. I missed my parents and Israel fiercely.

Just as I hadn't thought of the drain of speaking in English all the time, I also never realized how that seven-hour time difference could make me feel so far away. I could never just pick up the phone to call anyone back home. By the time I started my day, theirs was half over. By the time nightfall came to Virginia, it was nearly time for the sun to rise in Israel. It made everyone seem disconnected. I was sleepy when they were wide awake. They were settling in for bed when I left for my afternoon classes. I always had to pause for a moment when I picked up the phone to do the math. Could I call them right then? Did I have to wait until tomorrow?

My father called the morning after Payton moved in, wanting to know how things had gone.

"Things are good," I told him. Payton was out and the room was blessedly all mine. "Classes start in a few days. My roommate's parents took us out for dinner last night."

"And? Do you think you'll get along?"

I thought for a moment. "I feel like I could be her mother. She seems so young, *Abba*, you can't believe it. She told me last night she was scared to come here. She thinks it's dangerous to walk home alone at night from the library." I rolled my eyes and waited for him to chuckle, to shake his head at this child's silly fears.

He didn't say anything.

"This town is small," I clarified. "She grew up here."

My dad was quiet.

"What?"

"Maya, not everyone has had the experiences you've had." I could hear how carefully he chose his words. "For most people, going to college is a big change. Remember how you felt before boot camp? Leaving her home, sharing a room, needing to make new friends—those things are always difficult. And if she's always lived in one place and never been away—that just makes things harder for her, not easier. You shouldn't be so harsh."

"But—"

"You know I'm glad you're there. I think going to school is the right thing for you. I don't want to see you ruin it by being so judgmental. I can hear it in your voice that you're feeling superior." I gritted my teeth. I wanted to say that I had lived through and seen things these children couldn't even dream of, but I bit my tongue. "Just try to be patient with her," he said. "Try to view it from her perspective, not yours."

I didn't answer him.

"I don't want to fight over this." He sighed. "It'll be easier for you if you go easy on her. Don't push people away."

"Fine."

"Just remember you wanted to come to the States to be with people who haven't been through what you've been through. If you wanted hardened survivors, you could have joined Tikkun Olam and volunteered in Nepal. They have teenagers there who've lived through poverty and cruelty. But you wanted someplace safe, someplace soft. You can't be upset when that's what you find."

"Fine."

He sighed again.

"*Ima* wants to talk to you."

"Hi, *motek*," my mother's cheery voice came on. "How are you?"

"Fine." That was my word and I was sticking to it.

"What's wrong?"

"Nothing. *Abba* seems to think I already need a lecture on how to behave after sharing a room for one night, but besides that, everything is great."

"Maya," she scolded. "Honey, don't be so sensitive."

It had always been the case that my mother could scold me and it didn't upset me. But let my father say I needed to do something differently and if I were a rattlesnake, my rattles would be shaking out "*La Cucaracha*."

"It's not fair," I said. I could hear the whiny tone in my voice. "I'm two continents away from you guys, and then on our third phone call he gives me a lecture on how to behave!" Where did this clingy, whiny person I'd turned into come from? Even I didn't know.

My mother was silent on the other side of the line.

"*Motek*, I know this is hard for you. *Abba* knows this is hard for you too. But nobody forced you to go. You won't be doing yourself any favors pretending otherwise."

She stole my wind. With my sail of righteous anger emptied from under me, I was lost. Ridiculously, I felt tears well up.

"I miss you," I said.

"I miss you too. *Abba* misses you. We'll come up and see you soon. Maybe at the end of December, for Hanukkah. How does that sound?"

"Good," I sniffed. I wondered where I would go for Rosh Hashanah, or for Yom Kippur. I'd always spent the holidays with family. Always.

"So we'll see you in three months. Once your classes start and you get busy, it'll fly by."

"Yeah."

"We'll call you tomorrow at the same time, okay?"

"Okay."

"All right. I love you, Maya."

"I know, *Ima*. I love you too."

I hung up the phone.

So maybe I shouldn't laugh at Payton's fear of coming to UVA. I was two years older and still had plenty of my own issues to work through. I could be so tough and ignore so many things until I talked to my parents. Then it was like I was six years old again and terrified of the first day of school.

I didn't see Payton again until that afternoon, but when she finally showed up, I suggested we go to a local café and have an iced latte.

We walked through the muggy heat and settled down with a sigh in the air-conditioned café at a table by the window. Payton knew the girl behind the counter and followed her recommendations, ordering what was basically a coffee milkshake with vitamins, a new sort of drink that was very popular. I ordered an old-fashioned iced coffee and enjoyed the artistic swirls the cream made as it worked itself between the ice cubes down to the bottom.

"We went to school together," Payton told me, eyeing the counter girl. "We were best friends in fifth grade." She shrugged. "Now I barely know her."

"People change."

"Yeah, but it wasn't like that." She picked up on my condescending tone. "I pulled away from her. It's like one day I woke up and decided I just didn't want to be friends anymore."

I sat up and started paying attention. "Why?"

Payton looked embarrassed. "My parents were going through a hard time. Everything's fine now," she said quickly. "But when I was young, my mom was sick a lot."

"Sick" could mean a lot of things. I wondered what went wrong.

"I just didn't want anyone to know. I didn't want friends coming over. I didn't want anyone feeling sorry for me. It's pretty easy to drive friends away. Kind of sad, really. A part of me thought she'd stick by me, you know." She laughed a little, to show how silly she'd been. "You can't expect too much from people, especially kids."

"What was wrong with your mom?"

Payton looked surprised for a moment, but answered me. "She's bipolar."

"Bipolar?" I didn't know the word.

"You know, manic-depressive. I was ten when she was diagnosed. Then it took a while for them to get the meds right. Plus she wouldn't always take them."

"Oh."

"Yeah, I know. It freaks a lot of people out. I was ashamed of her all through junior high, most of high school. It took me a long time to realize it wasn't about me, you know? She wasn't doing it to hurt me. That's what I mean with this girl too. I kept wanting to think it was about me. If she were a good enough friend, she'd stick by me. If my mom loved me, she'd stop flipping out." Payton smiled, and I didn't think she looked so young anymore. "It doesn't work that way. Other people's lives don't revolve around you, you know?"

Unless you do something bad enough, I thought, but I didn't say it. I knew what she meant. It was true for most people.

"You're very honest," I finally said. "I'm surprised you'd tell me something like that."

She laughed a silly, infectious giggle and blew the image of world-weary wisdom.

"I know. You looked a little shocked. I'm kind of surprised to hear myself talk like that. I don't usually turn every conversation into a therapy meeting."

"I believe you. We're going to get along just fine," I said. Because I finally saw that under that blond hair and the wide eyes lay a real person.

She smiled. "I told you the minute I saw you. So what do you think about getting an area rug for our room?"

We talked about stupid things for a surprisingly long time. Even more surprising was how easily the conversation flowed. I expected her to grill me about my time in Israel, I expected her to complain about how hard it was to get organized, to deal with the cramped, hot dorm room, but it seemed I had not given Payton enough credit. After an hour, we felt revived enough to brave the heat again.

Damn it, I thought as I picked up my bag and returned my glass to the counter. My dad was right.

"I don't know how I'm going to survive this humidity," I said. We'd been walking for only a few minutes and I was covered in a sheen of sweat.

"I know," she said, though she didn't look at all bothered

by it. "It won't last much longer, you'll see. By mid-September the worst will be over."

"Israel has dry heat," I said, trying to justify my frizzled, sweaty condition. "It's much different. Hotter but easier to take."

I caught her glancing at me at the mention of Israel. But again, she didn't say anything.

"I came here straight from there," I said. For some reason, the fact that she didn't ask about Israel made me want to talk about it. "That's why I came a little early, so I would have time to get over the jet lag and learn my way around."

She nodded.

"I served in the military there." Why was I so chatty? Maybe I felt I owed her some information after she opened up to me. Maybe I was afraid of questions. "I served for twenty months, which is how long mandatory service is for women."

She nodded again, like she knew all about it.

"I bet your parents were so proud."

"Proud? No. Not at all. It's nothing special to serve in the army. Everybody does it."

"Weren't they scared you'd get hurt?"

"Women tend to stay in safe assignments. That's starting to change, but usually you don't have to worry about it. When my brother goes, that'll be a different story."

"Wow," she said. "That's so amazing. You've already done so much with your life. I feel like I haven't done anything compared to you."

"Don't kid yourself." I shrugged. "It wasn't glamorous or

exciting. It was dull and boring and just like having any other office job. Anyway, when my time was over—" I paused, not sure what to say. "I decided to study abroad. See the world." Liar. But she wouldn't understand. I didn't want her to think badly of Israel, to get the wrong idea.

"And here you are."

"And here I am."

Once orientation was over and classes began, I settled into a routine fairly quickly. Coffee in our room at seven, electric kettle, instant coffee powder, instant creamer, as Payton and I both got dressed for our eight o'clock class. I had class from eight to eleven most days. Then I went to an early lunch (to beat the crowds) and then to the library, or my favorite garden if the weather was nice, to read my assignments and do my homework. Reading took me a lot longer than it did most students, and I never went anywhere without my Hebrew/English dictionary. Payton and I usually met for dinner at seven, unless she had other plans.

A part of me had truly believed that all my friends were in Israel, and that nothing here could ever compare. I didn't talk much with the other students in my class—I would hurry by them as they mingled and flirted after class. I had nothing to say, nothing to share. We didn't have anything in common.

Three of my classes were lecture-style, so students weren't expected to raise a hand and participate. In my astronomy lectures, all I had to do was sit back and listen. But two of my classes were smaller and I really had to focus, to follow the discussions and think on my feet so I could say what I wanted to say. It was frustrating at first. I knew what I wanted to say, I knew how to say it in Hebrew, but I had to rethink the whole thought in English. It always came out wrong, either childish or incorrect, and I hated it.

I would practice with Payton, explaining to her what I had tried to say in class, and she helped me figure out how I should have said it. I was still surprised to see Payton and me become friends. Sometimes I'd catch sight of her walking and she didn't seem real, her perky nose and flowery sundresses belonging to another world. Then she'd see me and wave broadly, calling me over. I didn't come prepared for friendship.

"There's this guy you have to meet."

We had found a small table in the back of the cafeteria and were both toying with the remnants of Italian Night.

"Oh no," I said. "Do *not* try to fix me up with anyone." The very thought made my stomach turn.

"I didn't mean it that way," she said. I rolled my eyes. "Really! I think this guy even has a girlfriend."

"Oh, that's much better. What is that word—*polygamist*? Is that it?"

"I think that only counts if he's married to more than one person, not dating more than one, but that's beside the point. Will you listen?"

My gaze had drifted away.

"This guy, Chris, was in the Marine Corps. And I was telling him about you and how you were in the Israeli army and he wants to meet you." She smiled sweetly. "He's really nice. Besides, you need to get out more, meet some people. All you do is study all day."

I opened my mouth to defend myself, to tell her I was perfectly happy with the way things were. I came here to study, not "meet new people." But before I could say anything, she waved to someone behind me. I turned to look.

He had a crew cut and what I'd come to recognize as a football player's neck—as wide as it was long. He looked like a bodybuilder. I edged away.

"Chris," Payton said. "You found us. Grab a chair."

Chris, all two hundred and twenty pounds of him, obeyed her like a lamb.

"Chris, this is my roommate, Maya."

He sized me up and seemed slightly surprised by what he saw.

"Nice to meet you," he said in an unexpectedly high voice.

"Hi," I said. We shook hands. It was awkward.

I thought that Payton would leave us, inventing some meeting she had to rush to, but I underestimated her. She stayed with us, helping the conversation along when it faltered, charging ahead by herself when neither Chris nor I could think of a single thing to say. He seemed too embarrassed to ask me much of anything, and I was infected by his shyness and couldn't think of anything I might want to know about him.

By the end, though, Payton was victorious. She got him to tell us about enlisting in the marines, about his girlfriend and his folks, who lived in Blacksburg, Virginia.

"The marines are paying for this," he said. "They might even pay for law school."

"I wish my army would pay for this," I said. "They barely paid enough to buy food."

"Really?"

I shrugged. "It's different there, not like here. The army's just something everyone does after high school, it's no big deal."

"I wouldn't say it's a big deal here," he said. "But I did get a pretty sweet deal."

"Chris has been stationed in Japan," Payton said, nudging him. Chris obliged her and told us some stories about his six-month stint on Okinawa.

In the end, somehow, Payton arranged for Chris and me to start running together on Tuesdays and Thursdays.

As we walked back to our dorm room, I looked at her bemusedly.

"Are you always like this?"

"Like what?"

"Like a brigadier general, marshaling everything and everyone to do what you want them to do?"

"What?" She threw an almost perfectly innocent look my way. "I surely don't know what you're talking about."

"Deny it if you want to, but I know what you did back there."

"I don't—" she began, and then sighed. "You should get out more . . . you're like a hermit in our room."

"Thanks."

"No, no." She touched my shoulder. "I don't mean it in a bad way. I was imagining what it must be like to be in a strange place and I wanted to help out. Maya, you're not angry, right?"

Some days I felt like I could be Payton's mother, she was that young and naive.

"No, Payton," I said quietly. "I'm not angry with you at all."

Two weeks into classes, my huge history seminar was divided into smaller sections, each with a graduate student as its leader. In the section, we'd discuss points brought up during the lecture and each hand in three essays and one longish paper on a topic to be assigned.

I walked into the smaller classroom and found a seat in the far corner with my back to the wall. I studied the students filing in. Most were not first-years, as freshmen here were called, which was good, since hanging around eighteen-year-olds made me feel old and used up. On the other hand, it meant that these students had more experience with this sort of discussion, and I wondered if I would get my butt kicked on the grading. Every time I said anything, my accent gave me away: I didn't belong here.

They all settled down in their seats, hauling out notebooks and textbooks and looking prepared to defend their theses. Two minutes before class began, in walked our fearless leader, the graduate student who would lead us down the path of right conclusions and critical thinking.

At first I thought that maybe all graduate students looked

alike, bought their clothes at the same shabby-yuppie store, had the same careless haircut that flopped over their eyes. But as he opened up his satchel, brought out the class textbook, and looked at us, I realized that he wasn't a carbon copy. He was the same guy in the coffee shop from four weeks ago. What was his name?

"Justin Case," he said. I nearly jumped. Just in case what? I wanted to ask. "I'll be your section leader. Let's have everyone go around and introduce ourselves. We're going to be spending a lot of time together, we might as well know each other's names." He had a very smooth way of talking, comfortable in front of the class. I had a feeling he'd be a good instructor.

We all said our names, one by one. I hadn't done this since my parents sent me to sleep-away scout camp the summer after sixth grade. At least I didn't need to think of an animal that starts with the same first letter of my name. Maya monkey. Maya manatee. Maya mamba snake. Deadly, poisonous, and fast.

"Maya Laor," I said. He hadn't noticed me until then. His eyes widened slightly. He remembered me.

He handed out a schedule for the semester: due dates for papers, office hours, discussion topics in the upcoming weeks. Then he discussed what he expected from us and what we could expect from the class.

After class ended, I gathered my notes. On my way out, he called my name.

"Can I speak with you for a moment?"

The other students shuffling out the door looked at me

curiously. I wondered if they'd noticed anything during class. There was something about Justin. I kept looking at him, analyzing, trying to figure out what it was about him that both irritated and fascinated me. He had one of the most perfect faces I'd ever seen on a man. Straight, narrow nose, perfectly centered between gray eyes and above firm lips. I was more than a little disturbed by the thought that I wondered what it would be like to kiss him. I walked over to his desk feeling slightly ill.

"This is a surprise."

"Right. Small world."

"You said you were from Greenland, wasn't it? Settling in okay?"

I studied him closely. His face seemed open, his question friendly, but there was that glint of amusement that told me he wasn't buying any of it.

"I'm fine."

Pause. I knew I was being a bitch. I didn't know why.

"What year are you?" he asked. Maybe I wasn't the only one in the grip of an uneasy fascination.

"First." I tried to keep my face blank, but it was hard. He clearly wanted to keep asking questions, but good manners prevented him. "I'm not eighteen, if that's what you were wondering."

He saw I was laughing at him. He smiled. He had a nice smile.

"Somehow I didn't think you were fresh out of high school."

"Nope, I'm fresh out of the army."

"The army?" he said. "In Greenland? I didn't realize they had an army."

"Doesn't everyone have one?"

Then he smiled again, and I smiled back before I realized it.

"Welcome back to the civilian world." He rose from his seat, and again I was struck by how tall he was. He was one of those people you didn't realize were big until they stood near you. I took a small step back. "I'm glad to have you in my section. I think you'll be able to bring in a different perspective that will make the class much more interesting. Obviously the military has played an extremely important role in the history of the twentieth century." He zipped up his bag and put on the strap diagonally across his chest. "It'll be interesting to have a former soldier sharing her opinions."

"Yeah," I said, eloquent as ever.

We walked out of the room together.

That night, I couldn't fall asleep. I kept thinking about Dov. I thought about the first time we kissed, sitting on a blanket near his father's jeep in that dusty field. My heart hammering under my shirt, wondering if he could see it leap, it felt so wild. I could picture him clearly with that half-grin of his. I could hear his voice. How could he be gone? It seemed impossible, a stupid joke that I shouldn't fall for.

I listened to Payton breathe. She was almost invisible under her sky-blue bedspread. Only the top of her head showed, resting on a white pillow that nearly glowed in the dark room.

Finally I got up, pulled on a pair of jeans, and tucked in the large T-shirt I slept in. I grabbed my sandals and crept out of the room.

I walked for nearly two hours, aimlessly. It was a warm night, but cool enough to be comfortable. I tried to pick out the Big Dipper or the Summer Swan, but the sky was hazy and the clouds kept shifting. The stars were the same as in Israel, the same constellations I once pointed out to Dov, but I couldn't see them. There was nothing here from home for me to hold on to. Home felt light years away. Looking at the ground as I walked, I couldn't make out the sidewalk. There was only darkness under my feet.

I picked up my pace, nearly running through the dark and quiet streets. I thought these memories would fade once I got here. I thought they would diminish once classes began. But they hadn't. They were still here with me.

I was beginning to think they would always be with me, wherever I went, whatever I did.

Chapter Four

ISRAEL

I finished my one-week course in office administration, and I wasn't terribly surprised when I received my assignment. Whether Aunt Hen had pulled strings or whether it was just good luck, I was assigned to Rishon Lezion, a large base near Tel Aviv.

Once I moved into Hen's apartment, I quickly discovered that she was rarely there. I would catch a quick glimpse of her in the morning swallowing the last of her coffee and rushing out the door, and then I wouldn't see her until late at night. She saw many of her clients at dinner, and afterward she returned to the office to work on what they had discussed, which meant she usually didn't come home until nine or ten.

I realized that I had only ever seen Hen on her time off, when she was lounging, sipping a drink, taking it extremely easy, and I'd always believed that she was not a hardworking person. Now I saw that she was such a slow-moving slug during her downtime because she had so little of it.

Hen had three bedrooms in her apartment. Since her bedroom had its own bathroom, I had the hall bathroom and shower all to myself, something I'd never had before. Hen's kitchen was large, with pale cabinets that hid the oven and fridge. It was very modern and sharp and clean. It was also very empty.

That first morning, after saying a sleepy good-bye to Hen in her purple business suit and towering heels, I stumbled into the kitchen looking for breakfast. All I found was some instant Nescafé powder, no sugar. The fridge held a carton of milk, greenish cheese, and a shriveled little pear. Clearly, Aunt Hen was not putting on her hated pounds at home.

I made myself a cup of coffee and wrote a grocery list as I nursed it, making a face at its watery bitterness. But there was no time to do anything about breakfast now. I put on my uniform, assessed it in the mirror, and still felt a small thrill to see a soldier staring back. I practiced making a blank face so that I looked tough and unapproachable, then headed off to my new office.

I caught a bus and tried not to think about my stomach when the bus stopped by a bakery and the smell drifted in through the open windows. Cruel, just cruel. I told my stomach to stop whining. You're in the army now.

Every morning I'd get up, get ready for work, walk three blocks, catch two buses, and stand in morning formation. After work, I'd catch two buses back home, walk three blocks, enter a quiet and empty apartment, and eat dinner alone in front of the television. Once a week I had overnight duty and I spent the night on the base in a barracks room with three other girls. Irit and Leah were both stationed nearby and we managed to see each other, though usually only on Friday nights. When Irit came, she spent the night with Leah or me, since she lived over an hour away. Most nights I was in bed by ten, out of it by six. It was my first taste of true privacy and solitude. My first taste of loneliness.

Aunt Hen didn't have nearly as many glamorous parties as I'd always imagined. In two months she only had two functions, and I tagged along for one of them. It was a hugely boring affair and I finally understood why my parents were not more impressed with her lifestyle. It was glitzy, true, but deathly dull and more an extension of work than I had pictured. Conversations buzzed around a certain merger and one red-faced CFO who was caught in an extremely embarrassing situation with his young male assistant. As soon as people heard I was still a soldier, they'd ask me where I was stationed and what I was doing, and then pat me on the head. Sometimes literally.

In my third month at work, I stepped out of my cubicle and into the makeshift kitchen so that I could take my headache pills without any badgering from my co-workers. I had developed chronic headaches, dull and steady behind my right eye. There was someone in the kitchen heating leftovers in a dingy plastic container, and when he saw me choke down the pills he looked mildly concerned. I rummaged through the communal fridge to prove that I didn't just skulk into the kitchen to take medication (which I did) and found an apple. I wiped it on my shirt in a halfhearted effort to clean it.

"Do you want some?" he asked, tipping his head at the

rotating container in the microwave. "If that's all you brought for lunch, I have more than enough for two."

I raised a doubtful brow.

"Thanks, I'm fine." I showed him my apple. I didn't know who he was. He looked about my age, maybe a couple of years older because he was an officer, and you had to have been in the army longer before you could be one. He was tall and very dark, so that his blue eyes were almost startling when you looked him full in the face. If I hadn't felt slightly cornered, I would have thought he was cute.

"You might be having headaches because you aren't eating right."

"How did you know I had a headache?"

"You keep rubbing your right temple," he said.

I dropped my arm.

"You're too skinny."

I narrowed my eyes at him. Sometimes officers let their responsibilities go to their heads. I was not about to let him order me to gain weight. I did notice that he had nice hands, broad across with long, tapering fingers. It was almost a shame he was so annoying.

"Who are you, my mother?"

He started to smile, stopped, tilted his head, and looked at me. Finally he stammered a bit, cleared his throat and said, "What I meant to say was, do you want to go out sometime?"

Well, that was rich. "Do you even know my name?"

"Sure." He shoved his hands in his pockets and rocked

back on his heels. "You're Maya Laor, you work for Lieutenant Colonel Beral, and you've been here for a couple of months, plus or minus a few days." He grinned and his eyes crinkled so that only a wedge of blue showed.

Had he been spying? The movie I'd watched the night before was all about a charming but demented stalker.

"How do you know who I am? And who are you?"

"Dov Morelan. I work with intelligence one floor down. Don't freak out. I saw you walk to work a few times, asked around, and found out. You don't exactly blend in with the crowd." That was an odd compliment. Did he mean that I was pretty? Or just strange-looking? "I've been having lunch here all week, but this is the first time I've seen you."

"I usually skip lunch."

"Then no wonder you're downing pills like candy. Come on, let me take you out."

"Thanks, but no thanks." The weird thing is I was tempted.

He followed me to my desk and leaned a hip against it.

"So what are you working on?"

"Can't you take a hint?" I asked in disbelief. He looked very comfortable there, leaning against my cluttered desk. I tried to look cold and uninterested, but he was cute. He could also get in a bit of trouble, a lieutenant flirting with a private. I could feel people staring at us.

"What?" he raised his hands as if I held him at gunpoint. "I'm just being friendly."

"I'm not interested." I tried to talk quietly, but I knew I was going to get ribbed for this no matter how softly I spoke.

Good-looking officer, not from our floor, asking me out? Oh yeah, I was going to get a lot of grief for this.

"Who said I'm interested?" he asked.

"You asked me out to lunch."

"That was out of pity, sweetheart."

"What?"

The fact that I just squeaked like a mouse wasn't a good thing. The fact that he threw his head back and laughed wasn't so good either. "Kidding. I'm just kidding."

I couldn't help it. I laughed.

"You're impossible."

"I've been told." He straightened off my desk and winked. "See you around, Private Maya."

"Sure, whatever." But I turned back to my computer and had to fight a silly grin that kept wanting to take over.

Not quite love at first sight, but that was me, I guess. Give me a glass slipper and I'd twist my ankle and shatter the shoe.

The first time we went out for lunch, a week after our first meeting, Dov ordered for me before I had the chance. When he saw the look on my face, he had the good grace to look a little abashed.

"I hope that's all right with you," he said. "I come here a lot, I know what's good."

"Next time a simple recommendation will be fine." I was torn between anger and laughter. "Tell me, did you ever go to flight school?"

"No, why?"

"Because the only people I've ever met who are as arrogant as you are pilots. Do you usually order for people?"

"Only when I'm trying to impress them."

"Well, stop it. Because if you order my dessert, I'm leaving." I meant to sound peeved, but he just laughed and I was surprised to find that I found it funny too.

When the waiter came back, before Dov could say a word, I ordered two coffees and two desserts. He leaned back in his chair, arms crossed behind his head, and smiled.

"I knew you were going to do that," he said.

"And I knew you knew," I said sweetly. "But I decided to do it anyway."

He burst out laughing. I returned to the office in a better mood than I'd been in for weeks.

I didn't want to tell anyone about this date. It didn't seem to mean anything yet, and I didn't know enough about him. If he was a player or had already dated everyone else in the office, I didn't want to be made fun of. But gossip spread in the office like mold on damp bread. Just because I didn't tell anyone about it didn't mean people hadn't noticed.

"Maya, you dog!" Ilana caught my arm as I walked down the hall. "How long were you planning to hide it?" Ilana, with her hennaed hair and love of heavy gold jewelry, was my age, twice my weight, and half a head shorter. She was also better informed than the Mossad.

"Hide what?" For a moment I really didn't know what she meant.

"'Hide what?' she asks," she scoffed, and laughed loudly. "I'm talking about the fact that you tried to hide that amazing piece of flesh drooling after you. We're all ready to melt from those looks he sends you. I don't know how you do it, honey, three months in Tel Aviv and you've got the hottest man in the building after you."

We were just standing out there in the hall. Anyone could walk by and hear her. I could feel my face heat up.

"Do you mean Dov?"

"Who else?" She mocked. "Who else could I possibly mean?" She leaned in. "I hear he's unbelievable in bed. You're in for a good time." Her face was so near mine that I could see where her dark lip liner veered off her lip like a blip on a heart monitor.

I was embarrassed, annoyed, and just a tiny bit flattered that I was dating such a catch. But annoyance won out.

"That's disgusting," I said. "Besides, I thought you tried out everyone in the building. How great can he be if you haven't slept with him yet?"

She blinked in surprise.

"I've got to run," I said. "See you later." I took off before she could say anything. Ilana laughed behind me and I wanted to kick myself. My mouth, I swore, was not always connected to my brain. After she stopped laughing, I could feel her staring at my retreating back, speculating.

That Friday night, I waited at the crowded bus station for my bus to arrive. I was meeting my high school friend Daphna in South Tel Aviv, where most of the pubs and clubs were. Dov was going to be there. I was jostled forward as a mother and daughter brushed by me. People stood closer here in Tel Aviv than in Haifa, bumping, touching. I had almost gotten used to it.

I had spent nearly two hours getting ready, blasting U2 on my CD player, practicing my dance moves in the mirror. I finally settled on low-slung black pants and a dark-red shirt that rode high, exposing my navel. I had recently invested in half a dozen thongs and two push-up bras—things I never paid attention to in high school. But living with Aunt Hen was an education. She might rarely be at home, but when she was, she noticed things, whether it was water spots on her marble counters or a faint stain on my favorite white shirt. She was the one who had pointed out that my panty line was showing the last time I'd worn these pants.

"It's embarrassing," she said. "You don't want people to be able to see your underwear, you want them to guess."

"Guess what?"

"Is she or isn't she wearing any?"

"Ha, ha."

She lifted her brows. "Trust me."

I hadn't gotten used to wearing thongs yet, though when I confessed to Daphna that I'd bought some, she swore they get to be more comfortable than regular panties. This was only my third time wearing one and I was very conscious of it. Also, my breasts were up higher than usual, pushing out, so when I looked down, I could actually see them rising out of my shirt. I felt very sexy but also slightly off balance. I didn't quite know this new person I'd become. I liked her, but I didn't know her.

As I waited for the bus, I shook out a cigarette and dug through my purse for my matches. I wasn't perfect at lighting a cigarette yet. There was a style to it, a way to do it fluidly, to look like a black-and-white photo from the forties. But I couldn't bring myself to practice in the mirror. That seemed a little stupid, even for me.

After losing two matches to the slight breeze in the open station, I was lit and glowing. I took a deep drag and blew out the smoke in twin streams from my nose, like a dragon. I didn't really like smoking yet, didn't like the way it tasted, but there was no better way to keep your hands occupied. My stomach was full of nervous butterflies and my heart was skipping just a little too fast.

Dov will be there tonight, I thought for the thirteenth time. Not because of me, but because he was good friends with Daphna's new boyfriend. Small world. Maybe. Or maybe he'd decided to come because he knew I would be there. My heart rate kicked up a little more and the cigarette trembled on its way up. Be cool. I tried to think of how Hen would handle him, but failed. Forget Aunt Hen. I tried to remind myself that he was chasing after me, not the other way around. I wasn't sure what I felt for him yet, but my stomach and my damp palms were telling me they knew exactly what they thought of him. He was sexy and fine and Ilana wasn't the only one who'd made some jealous little comment about him after our one lunch date.

The bus arrived just as I finished my excellent pep talk. I tossed my ciggie onto the ground, making sure to step on it and crush it out before climbing onto the bus, about as steady on my high heels as a rowboat tied to a pier. I found an empty seat midway down the aisle and plopped down, my mind full of fantasies and lectures and nervous excitement. Would we kiss? Would he try? Should I let him?

The bus pulled out with a lurch. There were people standing in the aisle and they all swung forward and then back again, like seaweed in a shallow sea pool. A young man sat next to me, looking out the window. He was dark-skinned and growing a wispy mustache that made him seem very young, probably a waiter or busboy coming home from work. I looked away from him and saw an older woman holding onto the strap above my seat. Her hair was covered by a black kerchief framing a round face with sagging jowls. She looked sixty, though she might have been younger. I could never tell when they were covered up like that. I was mildly surprised that no one had offered her a seat. Someone should have. I glanced down and saw her ankles were large and puffy above her tan-colored shoes. I looked at the people sitting down but with the exception of my seatmate and me, everyone else was older.

I stood up.

"*Giveret*," I said in Hebrew. "You can have my seat."

She sat down without hesitation, pushing me slightly with her bulk. I staggered and grabbed for the handhold she had just vacated. She mumbled something at me, maybe "thank you."

I had expected something a bit more grateful.

The waiter-boy turned and looked at me. I looked away. I suddenly felt foolish with my pushed-out breasts and sexy clothes. I reached up with my other hand and grabbed a pole for better balance, trying to ignore the fact that it made my shirt ride high above my waist. Most people just take a cab when they go out on Friday night, but I wanted to save the money. I was beginning to think taking a taxi might be worth the extra expense.

The bus stopped several times, and after ten minutes I found a free seat, which I wasn't about to give up any time soon.

The waiter-boy kept looking at me, but I ignored him. When the seat behind me opened up, he moved into it. I could feel his eyes boring holes in my back.

I turned in my seat and glared at him. "What do you want?"

He seemed slightly surprised. "This seat was open, I can sit wherever I want to."

"Well, stop staring at me." I was sure he would try some stupid pick-up line and I was already annoyed with myself for dressing this way.

"You did a good thing, giving up your seat." He wouldn't meet my eyes, staring fixedly at a spot near my right shoulder. The words were grudging, like he wished he didn't have to say them.

"Oh." Now I really felt stupid. "Thanks."

He got off a few stops later and I looked out the window until he passed. As the bus pulled away, I finally relaxed. My thoughts drifted back to Dov and his brown hair that looked so soft. I couldn't decide what I wanted to happen tonight. I hoped he was a good kisser. Would I find out?

I got off at my stop and hurried over to Leila, the pub where we were meeting. Of course, after scanning the crowded place, I realized I was the first to arrive. After working my way to the bar, I ordered a rum and Coke.

Leila was packed with tiny round tables that had four, five, sometimes six people crowded around them, drinking beer or cocktails, nibbling on the olives and peanuts that came to every table. The walls were painted a deep lilac with silver stars, comets, and solar-system swirls twinkling all around. I tried to see if they'd painted any real constellations, but it all looked random.

Someone came up and stood next to me at the bar.

"Hi, sweetie," Daphna yelled in my ear, and then she gave me a wet kiss on the cheek. "I'm late, I'm late."

"For a very important date," I said, but she didn't get the *Alice in Wonderland* reference.

"Everyone else is waiting outside. We can't get a table here so we're going someplace else. Are you going to finish that?" She pointed to my drink.

"All yours."

She downed it and we left.

Outside, Dov and Bar were waiting. Bar had just bought a tiny two-door hatchback, and he'd parked it up on the curb with the hazard lights flashing as they waited for us. Dov got out and tilted the seat forward so Daphna and I could get in behind him. I smiled and he smiled back. I brushed by him as I got into the car.

Bar had some sort of techno music blasting from his

speakers and was driving to the pulsing rhythm, veering around cars, hand on the horn.

"I can't watch," Daphna wailed, and buried her face in my shoulder. She smelled of something that wasn't her perfume. Seemed the party had started without me.

Dov turned and looked at her in amusement.

"What about you," he said. Our eyes met. "Scared?"

"I'd like to see my death when it comes."

"Ah. Brave and beautiful. I can respect that."

"That's a relief." I wasn't even blushing. Maybe because it seemed he was testing me.

He turned to face the front again.

"You're so mean to him," Daphna whispered loudly. I finally got a good look at her eyes. They were bloodshot.

"Did you smoke up?"

"Don't be mad," she whispered. "I want to have fun tonight."

"Daphna, are you insane?" I tried to keep my voice down. "What the hell were you thinking? You're in the army. Do you know how much trouble you could get into?"

"Maya, don't be a drag. I know everyone at the MP station. Even if I get caught, they won't book me. I'm totally safe." She snuggled in next to me, pushing my hair out of her way. "Tonight'll be great. Dov is such a hottie."

"Did you all get high before you picked me up?" It explained Bar's erratic driving. I knew that I probably sounded like my mother, which wasn't cool. But I wasn't happy with the thought of riding in the back of a sardine can whose driver was probably seeing clouds and butterflies drifting by. It was also disappointing that Dov did drugs. It changed my opinion of him.

"Just wait till you see this new club," she said, oblivious. "Bar knows the bouncer, otherwise we'd never get in. God, I'm starving. Honey—" she called out. "Stop at the next kiosk we pass. I'm so hungry I could pass out."

Bar swerved, slammed on the brakes, and jumped a curb, scattering the people loitering around a shacklike falafel stand. We got a lot of glares, and someone shouted, "You fucking maniacs." I hunched down in my seat.

Daphna shrieked with laughter. I loved her and we'd been friends since forever, but I hated it when she got high.

Bar got out, tilted his seat, and Daphna crawled out. She nearly fell and Bar caught her. She laughed and wrapped her arms around him. They kissed.

I looked away.

"So." Dov twisted to get a better look at me. "You ready to have a good time tonight?"

"Not as good a time as you guys, apparently."

"They were like that when I got here."

I ignored the relief sneaking through me. He didn't do drugs. So what? "Is he safe to drive? I don't want to ride with a driver who's going to mistake a stop sign for a grinning monkey."

"You want me to drive?"

I thought about it for a moment. There was something very sober and steady about Dov.

"Yeah, I do. But there's no way you'll be able to talk Bar out of driving. No way he'll let you. He's a maniac about his car."

"Is that a dare?"

I laughed. "Sure, if you want to make it into one. Let's see you do it."

He was out of the car before I finished. He walked over to Bar, who was kicking pebbles, waiting for Daphna to get her order. Dov threw an arm around Bar and said something. Bar laughed. They both looked over at me. I glared and looked away. When I looked back, Dov was talking again and Bar was nodding.

Dov returned to the car.

"Come on, you're moving up front."

"What? But there's hardly room back there for me and Daphna. How is Bar going to fit?"

"They'll figure out something."

I got out. Dov and I leaned against the hood while Daphna devoured her stuffed pita. Bar kept taking bites until she ordered him to get another one for himself.

"What about you?" Dov asked. "Hungry?"

"No. It's nearly midnight; I don't know how they can eat that greasy food so late. Makes me queasy just thinking about it." I made a face. "You have to tell me how you convinced him to let you drive."

Dov looked down at me, amusement playing on his lovely face. "Oh, it's no problem. You just have to know what cards to play." Which of course made me wonder even more what he'd said to put that look in Bar's eye.

The orange streetlight washed out the color of Dov's eyes and made them seem nearly clear. Leaning against the hood, he folded his arms across his chest and brushed against me. I tried not to jump. I felt the contact all the way down to my toes. I studied him from under my lashes. He was wearing black cargo pants and a silky gray T-shirt that molded to his body. Something shifted and tightened in my stomach.

Bar and Daphna staggered up to us, howling at some private joke. Dov opened the door and tilted the seat. Daphna crawled in first and Bar grabbed her butt. She shrieked and twisted, and Bar dove in after her.

Dov drove smoothly, staying mostly in the same lane, shifting around slower cars in a controlled way that made me feel much better about the night to come.

Once we arrived at the nightclub, we pushed through the small crowd waiting to get in until we reached the bouncer, who scanned the crowd with maddening insolence, choosing who would enter and who would wait. There were two security guards standing off to the side, checking people's bags and coats with a handheld metal detector. Both had sidearms.

"A club down the street got bombed last month," Bar said, leading us through the crowd. "The bastard packed his bomb with nails covered in rat poison. Killed nine people waiting outside."

I eyed the crowd around us. It was impossible to see everyone, to notice if anyone looked suspicious. All I could see were folks dressed for clubbing, waiting impatiently to be let in and let the party start. I shivered at the thought of nails flying through this crowd, ripping through arms and legs and made-up faces.

Daphna smacked Bar on the shoulder.

"Don't say things like that."

"Why? Because it's true? You think some terrorist is going to hear me?"

"Just stop, okay? It's not funny."

He shrugged, looking amused. I was elbowed sideways by the people pressed in all around us. I stepped closer to Daphna.

Bar's friend wasn't that tall, which was unusual in a bouncer. He stood, trying to look bored, his oversized arms crossed across his chest, but the gleam in his eye gave him away. He was enjoying himself.

"Yo, Max," Bar bellowed.

"Hey, hey, hey," Max grinned. "You made it."

"Sure."

Max eyed Daphna, lingering on her chest and hips. "Looking good," he said. Bar threw an arm around her and squeezed.

Max uncrossed his arms and moved the low gate that held everyone back. We walked in. The chosen.

Once inside the overloud dark club, my eyes adjusted and I could see that the hot new club was practically empty. We gave it nearly an hour, listening to Bar swear it would fill up soon, but it didn't.

"My friend owns a club not far from here," Dov shouted in my ear. "Let's try his."

"Fine, just get me out of here," I yelled back. "This place sucks."

Bar sulked during the quick car ride and kept saying the club had been packed last weekend. Daphna retreated into a self-protective vegetative state and didn't utter a word. Dov and I stayed quiet and let Bar vent. I was sleepy and tried to think of a good reason to just skip this next club and go back to Aunt Hen's to crash. It had been a long week. It was well past midnight. My ears were already ringing from the loud music in Bar's stupid club.

But Dov parked the car and I still hadn't thought of a graceful way to get out of going.

This new club was brightly lit on the outside and glowing with happy neon colors. The bouncers wore bright blue pants and sunny yellow shirts. I started perking up.

"Hi, Dov," one of them said as we pushed through the crowd waiting to get in.

"Hi. Is Asi in tonight?"

"Naw, he's taking it easy tonight. He might be in later. I'll tell him you're here if he gets in. We've got a great turnout tonight. You should have a good time."

"Great." Dov smiled. The guy stepped aside and let us all through.

As we entered, passing through an airport-like metal-detector gate, a stunning girl in a hot-pink wig and a periwinkle bodysuit handed each of us a plastic test tube full of liquid. Mine was red, Dov's was green, Daphna got orange, and Bar's was yellow.

"What's this?" I said. "It looks radioactive."

"Vodka, syrup, and food coloring." She smiled. "It's good. Trust me."

"Ladies," Bar announced, sulk forgotten. "Bottoms up."

We drank.

The music was pulsing, the beat was good, and the dance floor was packed.

"Come on." I grabbed Daphna's hand. "Let's dance."

I dragged her to the middle of the floor so that we were surrounded by bodies on all sides, and then we danced, trusting the guys would find us if they wanted to.

I danced for hours, throwing my arms, shaking my hips, and letting the skittering beat carry me on its back like riding a wave to the shore. I was vaguely aware that Daphna had left to find Bar, but the floor was full of dancers pressing against me and I didn't care if I didn't know them. I kept on dancing, mesmerized by my bare arms undulating in the flashing lights, illuminated for split seconds, bright green or glowing white.

My face was damp with sweat and my hair clung to it as I shook and shimmied and twisted away from the week that passed and the week to come and any unpleasant thoughts that tried to creep into my mind.

I felt large hands settle on my swaying hips. I turned around, sure it was some stranger who wanted to dance, but it was Dov. I looked at him through half-closed eyes, waiting for him to say something. He didn't. A new song started up and I danced to it, arms twisting in front of me like a belly dancer's, like I was casting a spell. He stepped closer.

He leaned in and I thought for a moment he was going to kiss me. I dropped my arms and grew still. But his mouth went past my lips to my ear.

"Bar and Daphna want to go home," he yelled.

Not what I expected to hear.

"Not yet," I yelled back, peeved. I danced out of his grip. "A few more songs."

I thought he'd leave, but he stayed with me and we danced together. He was a sexy dancer, coming up close, almost touching but not quite. My heart was thumping pleasantly and I realized I really wanted to kiss him. Or rather, I really wanted him to kiss me. I thought about leaning in, tilting my head back, giving him the unmistakable invitation to kiss me.

Then Daphna found us. Even in the dark club with its blinding flashes of strobe lights, I could see she looked bad.

"Maya," she whimpered. "I wanna go home."

Dov drove again, but Bar sat in the front seat and Daphna and I were once again together in the back. She fell asleep, her head heavy against my shoulder. Bar was out too, his head resting at a funny angle propped up against the window. It was strangely comfortable with only Dov and me awake in the dark.

"Where should I drop you off?" he asked quietly.

"My aunt lives on Levi Eshkol." It was one of the most chic streets in Tel Aviv, of course.

He nodded and was silent for a while.

"I hope you had a good time," he said.

"You know I did." I didn't feel like being coy. "You're a good dancer."

"You're not bad yourself."

"I love dancing." I looked out the window, watching the

streetlights smear by. I gently readjusted Daphna's head on my shoulder. "I just get away when I dance. It's the only time I totally relax."

He didn't say anything else for the rest of the ride. Maybe he thought I'd fallen asleep. My head was in the shadows. I was tired, but I liked watching him. I'd never seen anyone drive so smoothly.

He reached my aunt's building. He shook Bar awake so he could let me out of the car. I eased Daphna off of me and once I was out, she stretched out on the back seat.

Dov got out and walked me to the main door.

"I like dancing with you," he said, leaning against the doorframe as I dug for my keys. "We should do it again."

I looked up, hand still in my purse.

"Okay."

"Good." He smiled. "Okay." Then he leaned in and kissed me lightly on the lips. I stayed perfectly still. He straightened and I couldn't read the look on his face. He ran a finger down the bridge of my nose, the way you would to a child.

"Sweet dreams," he said, and headed back to the car. I watched him get in and drive away.

Yeah.

I found my keys.

Good. Okay.

I entered the building grinning. I wasn't tired at all.

Chapter Five

VIRGINIA

I crept back to bed from my walk near dawn, exhausted. When the alarm rang at seven, I woke up with a start, not knowing where I was. There was a moment of panic and then I saw Payton emerge from her bed like a butterfly out of its cocoon.

"Morning," she rasped, and swallowed.

"Hey."

I rubbed a hand over my half-numb face and tried hard to fully wake up.

I sat through my nine o'clock class, and when it was over I had no idea what the professor had said. It was raining outside, which made me even sleepier. The hems of my jeans had gotten wet on my way to class and they stayed damp and clammy against my ankles, irritating me every time they brushed against my skin. By the next class I was more alert and my pants were a little drier.

The professor stood at the podium in front of the auditorium. The hall quieted and the rustle of students settling ceased. "Stellar evolution," the professor began, "is crucial to stellar survival. If a star cannot adjust itself to a stable configuration, it dies. Sometimes with a whimper. Sometimes with a bang."

I wrote his key points in my notes. "Even a stable star must change. It cannot continue to produce the same amount of energy indefinitely. Its surroundings change. Its energy needs change. A star must be able to adapt. To handle change. Stars that cannot change die."

I wondered if it was that simple for people too.

By the time I had the discussion section with "Just-in-Case," my jeans were dry and I was functioning at nearly full speed, though still in somewhat of a foul mood. Justin called on me twice, forcing me out of a pleasant stupor in which I daydreamed about a warm bath and a long nap.

No one said anything profound during class. Justin asked if anyone thought the military had a private agenda during the Bay of Pigs incident.

"They probably did," I piped up.

"Why do you say that?" he asked, his look sharpening in interest.

I felt the class's gaze shift to me. I'd blurted that out without thinking. Justin nodded, urging me to speak.

"The military is bred for action," I said, hoping I'd say this right. "On the one hand, no one understands the cost of going to war better than soldiers, because they're the ones who actually put their lives on the line." I paused, looked at Justin, who nodded again in encouragement. "But on the other hand, generals don't like sitting around and feeling useless. Without an active engagement to justify their training, I think they start feeling restless."

"What about Vietnam?" someone asked.

"That didn't really gear up until after Kennedy," I said. "The generals only had Korea, and the fighting there ended years before. Maybe they felt it was time for something new."

A couple of people actually nodded their heads in agreement, and I felt a warm glow from finally saying what I meant to say.

"If we consider what Maya said to be true, what role does the president, the head of the military, play?"

Someone raised a hand.

The rest of the class went by pretty easily, and it was over by the fifth time I checked my watch.

As we were filing out, a slender blonde came in and started chatting with Justin. He was leaning slightly away from her, his arms folded across his chest.

When she noticed me eyeing her as I zipped my bag, she shot me a cool smile.

There was something about her smile that grated on my nerves. I didn't bother smiling back. I was thinking about taking a nap after class, trying to decide if it was worth skipping cafeteria lunch and wondering whether we had any apples in the room that I could eat instead. I hefted my bag and walked out, leaving the two of them alone.

As I pushed open the main doors heading back to my dorm room, I heard the metronome sound of the eaves dripping and it reminded me I left my umbrella in class. With a sigh, I turned around and trudged back to the classroom and walked in just as Justin was leaning in for a kiss. Her head was tilted back, eyes closed, lips ready for landing. But Justin's eyes were open and at the sound of my footsteps, hesitating at the door, he looked at me.

"Sorry," I said. "I forgot my umbrella."

They separated.

"Seems like you're always leaving things behind," Justin said, maybe to fill in the uncomfortable silence.

"Only when you're around." The devil made me say it.

He grinned, and Blondie narrowed her eyes.

"Maya," he said, remembering his duties as host. "This is Brook Maxwell. Brook, this is Maya Laor."

"Hey," I said.

"Nice to meet you." To her credit, she seemed only slightly embarrassed by all this.

"Right." I stooped down and grabbed my damp umbrella, leaving a wet smear on the floor. "Sorry to, ah, interrupt." I waved my umbrella. "See you next week in class." I hurried out.

"Wait, Maya," Justin called after me, and jogged out of the classroom.

She won't like that, I thought. I pictured a preppy huff. The thought of someone else having a bad day was so cheering that I smiled as Justin caught up.

"It's not what you think."

"What?" I blinked. "It's not my business. You don't have to explain yourself to me."

"I know," he said. "It's just that we used to go out. It's been over between us for months. What you just saw was a huge mistake . . . I'm glad you came in when you did."

"It must be difficult when beautiful women throw themselves at you. Hard to say no."

He actually blushed. We stood looking at each other for a moment. He took a deep breath.

"So in the interests of, ah—keeping a small world at bay, would you mind not telling the other students what you saw in there?" His ears were turning pink.

I couldn't help it. I grinned.

"Worried about your reputation?"

"You could say that. It's a pretty small community here. I just don't want people in my business."

I could certainly relate to that.

"Your secret's safe with me."

His shoulders relaxed slightly and I realized he'd been nervous.

"Thanks, Greenland," he said.

I laughed. "I'm not really from there."

"Oh yeah?"

"Yeah." I waited. "Aren't you going to ask where I'm from?"

He shrugged. "You'll tell me when you feel like it. If I ask again now, I won't know if you're telling the truth. If I wait until you tell me, then I'll know."

I wasn't sure that was a compliment. Why was I suddenly feeling uncomfortable, unable to meet his eyes?

* * *

It rained again, and by the time I got to my room, my shoes and the bottom third of my pants were soaking and muddy. Payton wasn't there. I dropped my bag in the corner and it slowly formed a puddle around itself, as if it were melting.

I dug out my fuzzy blue sweatpants and a pale-yellow fleece that always reminded me of the fluffy baby chickens from the kibbutz I visited as a child.

Israel never got much rain. It seemed like it got less and less every year. I associated the sound of rain—dripping from gutters and branches, plopping into puddles—with good things, good news. Though it was slightly disconcerting to have so much of a good thing now. I flicked on the electric kettle and found a packet of instant soup. Five minutes later, carefully drinking tomato soup from a mug, I sat on my bed and leaned against the wall.

In Israel, the main meal of the day was lunch. It felt right, balancing the day. But now, less than two months later, I was already on the American schedule. I tried to keep eating the big meal at lunch, but that meant I ended up eating two big meals a day instead of one. After gaining three pounds in two weeks, I stopped eating heavy at lunch. In yet another way, my life was different now than before.

I cradled the mug between my hands, letting the steam curl around my face.

It was seven hours later in Israel than in Virginia. The sun had already set, the workday was over. It was still hot there, the temperatures soaring during the day. Unfathomable.

The phone rang, too loud in the quiet room. It startled me and I nearly spilled my soup.

"Hello?"

"Maya? It's Chris Steward. I wanted to see if you were up for running this evening?"

"In the rain?"

"Sure. It's great running in the rain." He laughed. "My sergeant used to say 'It ain't training if it ain't raining.'"

I groaned.

"You should hear what else he said."

The last thing I felt like doing was getting wet again. While running.

"What time?" I asked.

"About eight?"

"Fine," I said, feeling more than a little masochistic. "Eight tonight."

"Great. I'll meet you in front of the O-Hill cafeteria."

I finished my soup, pulled up the covers, and went to sleep listening to the rain.

I woke up at four that afternoon to the sounds of shouting. I staggered out of bed, groggy, my limbs heavy with sleep. Outside my room, Yami was standing beside her overturned bucket. A dark puddle was spreading across the gray carpet of the common room. Tiffany, who lived two doors down from Payton and me, was holding a dripping notebook at arm's length.

"You did this on purpose!" Tiffany's voice, always excitable, was verging on shrill.

"Look." Yami, gruff as always, apologized to no one. "I have better things to do with my time than to make more work for myself cleaning up this mess just to get your notebook wet."

"Apparently you don't! Do you know how much work went into these notes?" Tiffany eyed Yami's work smock up and down. "I guess you don't."

I stepped out of my room.

"Hey, Tiff, everything okay?" I tried for a calming tone, but my voice was scratchy from sleep.

"No. It's not okay. Look what this person did!"

"Oh," I said. "Gosh. All your notes."

"I know!" She had no sense of sarcasm.

"You'd better start recopying what you can before the ink smears completely," I suggested helpfully.

"You're right," she said, her eyes growing big. She threw a hateful look at Yami. "This had better not happen again or I'll report you." She stormed out of the common room.

Yami's flared nostrils settled down and she shook her head.

"Tiffany likes being dramatic." I felt the need to apologize. "She's like that with everyone."

"You mean self-centered, oblivious, and neurotic?"

"Yeah."

Yami looked tired. Her skin seemed too large for her face and her hands hung limply by her side.

"Listen," I said impulsively. "I'm going to have a cup of coffee to wake up and you look like you could use one too. Can you take a break?"

She looked at me with an odd tilt of her head.

"It's just instant, but I have flavored creamer." It was something Payton introduced me to a few weeks ago and I was addicted.

"Sure," she said after a moment when I thought she would refuse. "I could really use a cup of coffee right now." She righted the bucket, left the puddle on the floor, and walked into my room. I closed the door behind us.

"It seems like every time you see me either I'm going to sleep or I just woke up. I don't usually sleep in the afternoon." I felt the need to justify myself. I twitched the covers back into place on my bed. "Go ahead and sit on the bed if you don't mind."

She sat down gingerly.

"Payton and I keep meaning to get some chairs." I filled the kettle up with bottled water and flicked it on. "But there isn't really any place for them. The desk chairs are really uncomfortable, we always just sit on our beds. I hope you don't mind." I got out two mugs and peered inside them discreetly to make sure they were clean.

"I don't mind."

"We don't have any sugar, but the creamer is sweetened."

"It's fine."

I smiled awkwardly, wondering why I kept apologizing.

When the water was hot, I fixed us the coffee and joined her on my bed, cross-legged, leaning against the wall. We sipped in silence.

"I've been working here for almost five years," she said after a few tentative sips. "Five years I've cleaned dorm bathrooms and hallways. And not once has any student invited me into their room."

I didn't know what to say.

"They think I'm some sort of servant. Some of them get mad that I don't clean their individual rooms." She sipped. "Sometimes—" She stopped and shook her head. "Never mind."

I stayed quiet.

"It just pisses me off," she said with heat. "They care about starving children in Africa, they fight to protect the spotted owl, but they don't have a clue. They think they're open-minded. They think they're good-hearted. They think they know how this world works. But they're just spoiled, entitled little brats who get drunk every chance they get."

I studied my warped reflection inside the half-empty mug.

"Some of them," I agreed. It was definitely what I thought of the students when I first got here. Now I wasn't so sure.

"Present company not included."

"I wasn't hunting for compliments."

"Fishing," she corrected.

"What?"

"You weren't fishing for compliments."

"Right."

"No," she laughed. "The phrase. The phrase is 'fishing for compliments,' not 'hunting for compliments.' "

"Oh. Whatever." I waved away her corrections. I'd made

so many mistakes already, that one was tame. "I once said, 'I wonder if there's any piss in the chicken' instead of 'any peas in the kitchen.'" I shook my head. "Now, *that* was embarrassing."

She laughed again, this time without any reservations.

"Why do you keep working here if you hate it?"

"It's a good job. It doesn't pay much, but I have good hours and it's usually easy since I won't clean vomit. The health care is great, and I guess I like working for a university. It's better than cleaning a big office somewhere. Besides, I'm not tied down. I could go anywhere, leave anytime I wanted to. It's easy to find another job."

"But you don't have to clean."

"You don't understand," she said, slightly hostile. "You think going to school, getting a good job, you think that's just part of your deal. That's what belongs to you. But it doesn't work that way for everyone."

I thought of Payton's schoolmate, the one who wouldn't stick by her. Everyone had a battle to fight, and it was easy to lose your way in the middle of the smoke and fire.

"There's night school, or community college. You could take computer classes, or maybe nursing school." I was pleased I could think of so many options off the top of my head. "There's plenty you can do that isn't as expensive as this university. We both know you're smart. Besides, I'm not from here. This is not part of my deal. Everyone back in Israel thinks I'm insane."

"It's just a job," Yami said. "It's not my life."

The door opened and Payton blew in.

"Oh, hi," she said, friendly as always. "I'm not interrupting anything, am I?"

"No." Yami stood up. "I'm all done here." She put her mug on the corner of my desk. "I need to get back to work." Right before she walked out the door she turned back. "Thanks for the coffee."

"Sure." But I was talking to an empty door.

"Was that who I think it was?" Payton said, closing the door.

"Yeah," I said. "Tiffany bitched at her for spilling water on her notebook. Said she did it on purpose."

"Tiffany's such a freak." Payton stripped off her wet shirt and added it to my pile of wet clothes. "I'm glad you apologized."

"Yeah," I said, and didn't bother to explain.

As I waited for Chris under the overhang in front of the cafeteria, I bobbed up and down on my toes to warm up and to get in the mood for a run when all I wanted to do was go back to my room, crawl under my warm covers, and read. The rain hadn't stopped, though it wasn't coming down as hard. I wondered if Chris would slow down because of me or keep speeding up to show how in shape he was. He seemed like a nice guy. My guess was he'd be careful about letting me set the pace.

When he arrived, we said our hellos and hit the road. My legs protested, as they always do. I could feel the tightness in my hamstrings and quads. Then came a mild burning. Finally, after nearly ten minutes of concentrating on my breathing, on striding out and rolling my feet, I found my rhythm. Chris was easy to run with. I thought at first that he might be measuring my stride, trying to gauge what sort of runner I was, but I stopped caring if this was his usual speed. We didn't talk much during the run. I could never talk and keep my breath even. One of the reasons I stopped smoking after my first few cigarettes was that I could feel tightness in my chest when I ran.

We ran up Observatory Hill, past the observatory, down into the main university area, through it, and back around.

"I like running at night," he said as we walked our cooldown. "I can't stand it when the sun's beating down, it just saps the energy right out." I liked listening to his drawl, but I found that I had to concentrate or I didn't catch what he was saying. There was a slight delay between the time he finished speaking and when I finally understood what he'd said.

"Yes," I said. "Me too."

"Kind of tough when you're in Israel, isn't it? I mean, not running when it's hot and sunny." It was the first question he'd asked about Israel. People seemed so restrained here. In Israel I'd be bombarded with questions. Where'd I come from, how'd I like it there, what did I think of it here. I could feel the curiosity shimmering off him, but unless I gave him an opening, he wasn't going to ask much.

"Sure," I answered easily enough, but I didn't encourage

him to ask more. "I tried to run in the early morning or in the evening, though I'm not an early-morning kind of person."

He gave the obligatory laugh. "Me neither."

The cafeteria was up ahead; we had come full circle. It was a good run, half an hour, six or seven kilometers. I tried to calculate that in miles. Just under four, I thought.

He looked at his watch. "Not bad," he said. "That was about seven-fifty per mile. Not my best time, but not my worst either."

"Me too," I said.

"Yeah?" he said, eyeing me. "Guess the Israeli army keeps its soldiers in good shape, huh?"

I shrugged.

"So, Thursday? Same time, same place?"

"Absolutely."

"Cool, see you then."

He trotted off into the darkness and I walked back to the dorm room for a hot shower. The rain had felt good while we ran, cooling me off, but now that I stopped running, I noticed how wet my clothes and hair were and I could feel the chill sinking in.

Standing under a strong, hot stream of water, I thought about why I hated to talk about Israel. It felt like a bruise, and I shied away anytime anyone stretched out a hand to touch it. I shook my head under the steady stream, sending water flying. There was no point in lying to myself. It was more than that. Israel was guilt. I was a hypocrite. I ran away because living there was unbearable for me.

Every time I thought about it, that feeling came back, that half-queasy sense of failure. It was my country. I still believed I would return to Israel. I had to come to terms with it or I would break. I couldn't live cut off from myself. But I feared my wandering mind. Anytime something reminded me of Israel, of Dov, my stomach would clench in pain, my heart would race, and I would feel nauseated. I cut off the water and stood in the shower stall, naked and dripping. I had to make it stop.

Payton was already in the room, sitting cross-legged on the bed, as I entered.

"How was the run?" She was wearing pale-blue cotton pajamas with white sheep. Her hair was up in a scraggly ponytail, already coming down around her face.

"It was good." I didn't feel like talking. I closed the door to our room and turned my back to her. I took off the robe and reached under my pillow for my boxers and shirt. I was tired, sapped to the bone.

"It can be hard sometimes," she said. "Being here, not having your own space. When I first came here I thought this place looked like a prison. Our rooms looked like cells to keep criminals in." She waved a hand to indicate the room, the building in general. "Actually, prisoners get a higher level of food quality in their cafeteria than we do." She shook her head at life's injustices. "The floors here are covered with gray linoleum. Why gray? The ceiling is low. We live under fluorescent lights. You know, when I first came here, I looked inside the bathroom and counted the showerheads and stalls.

Twenty girls to four stalls and four showerheads." She rolled her eyes.

I let her talk flow around me. Why was she was telling me this?

"I was so depressed. I found my assigned room and I tried the door and it opened, even though it's supposed to be locked." She rested her head on her knees. "I didn't think we were allowed into our rooms early. I looked inside. It was dark because the curtains were drawn. There was stuff all over the floor, like someone had started unpacking." I started paying attention. "Then I saw you sleeping on the bed." She laughed. "I felt like one of the bears returned home to find Goldilocks. Someone was sleeping in my room. And then you rolled over and mumbled something and I left."

"I didn't know you came in," I said, getting under the covers, shivering slightly. "Weird."

"I didn't feel like meeting my new roommate yet. I was sure I'd get to move in first since I lived so nearby. I'd planned to get here at seven so I could stake my bed, my desk, my side of the room. I was just stunned, you know? How did this person get to move in so early? I kicked the wall. You know that dark scuff between our room and Tiffany's? I did that." She looked like she had just admitted to a heinous crime. "It's funny to think about it now. I mean, everything worked out so well, and I like it here. But at the time it seemed just awful, like nothing was going to work out the way it should."

I was quiet and my eyes felt heavy. I wasn't sure what to say.

"I guess what I'm trying to say is just because something doesn't go the way you expected it to, it doesn't mean it won't work out in the end. Maybe even better than you thought."

I curled on my side and hugged a pillow to my chest.

"I'm fine, Payton. I'm just really tired right now."

"I know. I'm glad you went running with Chris, and I don't want you to think I'm meddling."

I smiled. "I don't. I think you're wonderful and sweet and I am really lucky that we're roommates."

She smiled brightly.

"I'm glad you said that," she said, and my heart sank just a bit because I recognized that tone. "A friend of mine is in ROTC and one of his instructors is married to an Israeli woman. So if you wanted to get together, I can get you her number."

"Oh."

"What? I thought you'd like to meet another Israeli living in town. Was I wrong? I thought you were homesick."

I was angry with myself for getting tied into knots at the thought of meeting another Israeli. I was annoyed with Payton for being considerate and thinking she could fix everything. But I held my tongue when I saw her face, hopeful, hesitant, and well-meaning. Instead of saying I wasn't interested, I forced a smile and, with as much enthusiasm as I could fake, said I'd love to meet her.

By eleven, Payton had finished her reading and turned out her light. I lay in bed listening to her breathe until midnight. I finally got out of bed, pulled on a cotton cardigan, slipped on my shoes, and crept out the door.

It was past midnight on a weeknight, and while the streets were not deserted, there was enough solitude for me to be able to walk in my boxers and not draw much attention. There was also enough silence for me to be able to think. The rain had stopped, but the roads were still wet and shiny under the streetlights. The trees dripped down on my head and shoulders.

Everyone said it wasn't my fault. They still said it. But I knew different. It was the reason I couldn't bring myself to go anywhere, to meet anyone those last four months. I couldn't take the responsibility. There were three bombings before I left, and each time I just felt weak with relief because it wasn't me. I had nothing to do with it. Not my fault.

But with Dov, it was.

A butterfly flaps its wings, the saying goes, and a storm breaks over the Caribbean . . . but what if you were that butterfly? Were you to blame?

I reached the top of Observatory Hill and sat on the steps of the deserted observatory. I shrugged in the darkness, fighting the urge to weep. He was gone. He was lost forever. Because of me. Because he loved me. How can love be worth that?

Where did that leave me?

Where was my home?

A part of me seriously thought about not going back to Israel. Would I rather stay here and be safe? Could I ever feel at home here? How could I not love Israel best? How could I ever live there again? Payton's sweet, naive idea that everything works out in the end was hopelessly not enough for me.

Even though I walked for another hour, avoiding the dripping trees and the metallic silver puddles, I found no answers. Finally I returned to my room, slipped into bed, and pretended to go to sleep.

Chapter Six

ISRAEL

"Come with me Friday night," Aunt Hen said. "The mayor will be there, and Yair Lapid." Lapid was a very cute journalist with his own talk show. "It'll be fun."

Dov had been swamped at work. He went to the West Bank for a series of meetings. I thought he would call about dancing again, but a week had already passed. I tried to get Daphna to tell me what Dov had said to Bar about Friday night, but she claimed to know nothing. She did say she thought he seemed interested.

"Sure, I'll go," I said, though I knew I wouldn't have a good time. But it was better than staying at home watching the news. "What should I wear?"

Hen smiled. "We'll go shopping."

I smiled back. Shopping with Hen was a distinct and happy pleasure. I had never been offered a cappuccino in a store before. I had also never had the shop assistant pick out the clothes for me, not even giving me the chance to browse around and see what caught my eye. They all knew Hen by name and learned mine, so that by the second visit they greeted me too.

They thought I was her daughter. She didn't correct them

and neither did I. I felt guilty for a moment, thinking of my mom, but decided we were all pretending here. They pretended they genuinely liked us. We pretended they had our best interests in mind when they suggested a particularly stunning dress. So I let Hen pretend I was her daughter; what difference did it make? I ignored the slight twinge that said maybe it was disloyal.

Before I came to Tel Aviv, I had a vague guess as to what Hen's chic wardrobe cost, but once I went shopping with her, I realized how far off I was.

I began to understand her irritation when one of my young cousins smeared her cashmere-beaded top with their grubby little hands. I started noticing seams and hems and the flow of material. I began to recognize designers and could sometimes tell an imitation from the real thing. I wasn't sure what good this would do me. As far as I could tell, I would never be able to afford such clothes.

My mother called and I told her about the party on Friday.

"I'll meet Yair Lapid," I said. "Want an autograph?"

"Don't you dare."

"I was kidding. I would never do something so embarrassing." Because Hen would kill me, but I didn't say that.

"I don't like this," my mother said. I could hear the censure in her tone.

"What?"

"You're developing this sort of sarcastic, condescending humor that I hate. Hen is trying to seduce you." I wondered at her choice of words. Seduce. "I don't know if this is the best thing for you right now."

"What do you mean? Hen is being great to me."

"I know."

"So what, you want her to be mean to me? To make me feel like this isn't my home?"

"Forget I said anything."

This was a classic tactic that never failed to annoy me.

"Fine. You shouldn't have said anything. So let's just forget it."

A little while afterward, as I cut some tomatoes and cucumbers for my dinner, I realized that this was the first time I'd ever taken Hen's side over my mother's. Maybe that was my mother's point. I scraped the vegetables into a bowl and shrugged in the empty kitchen. My mom was just jealous. I settled on the couch in front of the television, crossed my legs, and clicked on Yair Lapid's program. I'll meet him Friday, I thought with satisfaction. I ate my salad.

The party was at a seafood restaurant on the beach. It was all lit up and sparkling, and I wondered how much this party had cost. There was a huge buffet set up, loaded with food and jungle-sized flower arrangements. There were hunks of glistening meat on kebabs, golden puff pastries stuffed with ground meat and spices, endless bowls of summer salads, fruits, and baskets full of warm crusty bread. I filled a plate and chatted with Hen, but soon she saw someone across the room and hurried to speak with him about an upcoming case. Inevitably I found myself with an empty plate, strolling aimlessly, trying to look like I had some business being there.

A five-piece band was playing mambos and tangos from one corner, surrounded by lush plants. They were cranking out a saucy beat, but no one was dancing and it seemed like a waste. The volume of the conversation was growing louder as more and more people arrived and loosened up with drinks. I lost track of Hen. There was a huge crowd around Yair Lapid that I wasn't about to add myself to. Everyone fawned over him, laughing too loudly and adoringly. It seemed undignified. Even though Hen had told me that the mayor was coming, I didn't know what he looked like. I tried to guess which one of the many men mingling was the mayor, but it was useless and not very entertaining.

I strolled out to the balcony, figuring I'd wait out the party inconspicuously. As always, I was the youngest person in the room by a good decade. Why did Hen ask me to come with her? Maybe because she didn't have a date and you just couldn't walk in alone. Once through the door, however, she didn't need me. I was pretty miserable. I felt bad that I had been curt with my mom. She knew what her sister was like.

I was wearing a rust-colored halter top that I had borrowed from Hen. My hair, which Hen insisted I wear down, tickled the middle of my back and blew around my face in the ocean breeze. Hen bought me the pants I wore. Straight and black, they had a fringe of turquoise beads around the ankles that swayed when I walked. They were my payment for coming. Around my throat I wore a matching strand of tiny blue beads which I bought at the same store, even though Hen had offered to pay for them. I took off the necklace and used it to tie back my hair. It wasn't perfect, but the hair was out of the way. I leaned against the railing and listened to the waves crash.

It was cold out. But I was alone, and I preferred being cold and alone to being warm and fighting to blend in with the potted plants.

The balcony door opened. I kept my back turned, hoping whoever it was would leave seeing that someone was already out here. But instead, I heard footsteps approaching. I turned in exasperation, ready to ward off any attempt at conversation. Then I saw who it was and I froze.

"Hi, Maya."

"Dov?" For a moment I was confused. Had Daphna told him where to find me? "What are you doing here?"

"Same thing as you." He sounded amused. "Trying to escape death by boredom."

I laughed, suddenly glad to be out here. He wore a cream-colored linen shirt, and it blew around him, making him look like a hero on the cover of a romance novel.

"But why?" I asked. "Who dragged you here?"

"My dad. He runs an advertising company. My mom couldn't come tonight, so here I am. His date for the night, so to speak."

"Sounds familiar." He joined me at the railing. "I guess it's against the rules to come to these things alone, huh?" We both faced out, looking at the ocean, resting our elbows on the black metal railing.

"Guess so," he said.

"But then once you're in the door, forget about it. They don't need you anymore." I sounded a lot more bitter than I intended.

"You came with your aunt?" We were standing close and I could almost feel the heat coming off him. It was hard to pay attention.

"Yeah," I finally said. "She lured me here with a shopping trip and Yair Lapid."

Dov laughed. "You're easy. I get to use my dad's jeep all Saturday. You've got to learn to drive a harder bargain."

I kicked out a foot so he could see the beads around my ankles. "I'm happy with these, aren't they adorable?"

He studied my leg and then looked at me.

"Precious," he agreed. "Does that mean you won't go for a walk on the beach? You might ruin the pants."

What the hell, I thought.

"Easy come, easy go," I said. "Let's get out of here."

The next day, Dov picked me up in his father's jeep to go off-roading in some abandoned fields he knew about. I didn't know anyone else with a four-wheel-drive vehicle. Israel was mostly flat, parking was always tight, and gasoline was expensive. Everyone I knew had a small sedan. It seemed very exotic to be in a jeep, like we were on a safari. He picked me up in front of Hen's high-rise, and Hen, who was out there with me, flirted with Dov.

"How's your father?" she cooed, eyeing the jeep.

"He's at work. My mother says she feels like a concubine, coming in second to his first wife, the office."

"Faithful and sexy," Hen, madly in love with her office, agreed. "What more can you want in life?" She didn't give him a chance to answer. "Your dad bought you a jeep?"

"Oh no," Dov laughed easily, and I wanted to kick Hen. "He just lets me borrow it from time to time."

"We've got to go," I said. Hen was in my way and I couldn't get to the passenger door without nudging her aside.

"You be careful," she said, pulling on my braid like I was a child. "Take care of her," she warned Dov.

"Always," he said.

It took nearly an hour to get to where Dov wanted to go. I studied the rocky fields in front of us.

"You've done this before, right?" I asked as he edged the jeep off the paved road.

"Once or twice." He gunned the engine. "Ready?" He didn't wait for my answer. We were off. I grabbed the handhold above the door.

The jeep bucked and swerved, and Dov drove fast over the uneven ground.

I screamed every time we hit a ditch, the jeep tilting forward and to the side. I could feel the springs in my seat with each jolt. I was pretty sure I was coming home with whiplash.

"*Elohim!*" I screamed. "We're going to flip!"

Dov roared with laughter, though he didn't take his eyes off the road. "You haven't seen anything yet." He turned the wheel and we flew off in another direction.

"Your dad lets you do this?" I shouted over the roar of the overworked engine and the rush of the wind.

"Why do you think I agreed to come last night?"

Then he whooped and we went sailing over a small rise, airborne for a split second. I grabbed the handhold on the door and closed my eyes. My stomach caught up a few moments later.

He stopped the jeep and studied me. I opened one eye and looked at him. "Is it over yet?"

"Wanna try?" I could hear the dare in his voice.

"Are you serious?"

"Unless you don't think you can handle it."

"You think I can't?" I opened the other eye to fully appraise him.

"I don't know, can you?"

"What about your dad? It's his jeep, he probably wouldn't want me to drive it."

"Don't hurt the jeep and he won't know. But if you're scared . . . ?"

"Never. You're on." I unbuckled and we switched seats. Once behind the wheel, my heart rate picked up. "Are you sure about this?" I said again. The only car I'd ever driven was my mother's Citroen, a two-door hatchback. It was a stick shift as well, but it was nothing like this luxury four-wheel-drive cockpit.

"It's a rush. You'll love it." He buckled in with a click.

"Okay," I said, scooting up the seat, adjusting the rearview and side mirrors. "Here we go."

I drove us for half an hour. I wasn't nearly as daring as Dov had been, but I got us airborne twice, and I think I managed to scare him when I cut close to a tree. I felt very wicked and glamorous and it was the most exciting thing I'd done since I joined the army.

Finally we decided to stop and have lunch.

We sat on a couple of large rocks and Dov brought out the food his mom packed for us—sandwiches on bakery rolls, two oranges scored and ready to be peeled, a thermos with warm tea, and two yogurts.

"My aunt never has food in the house, I miss that." Most people lived at home when they served at a nearby base. I was jealous because living with Hen didn't feel like home. No one made my lunch or dinner anymore.

"I need to get out of my parents' house," Dov said. "Having someone make your lunch isn't everything."

"Just wait until it's gone. Then you'll miss it."

"I hate living at home. I'm twenty-two years old and living with my parents. It's killing me."

"But everyone does it," I said. "You can't afford to rent a place in Tel Aviv. What the army pays you won't buy you dinner for a week, let alone pay the rent."

I took a big bite out of the sandwich. It had cheese, tomatoes, and slices of hard-boiled eggs.

"I know," he said. "But it drives me crazy sometimes."

"I miss home. I miss my parents."

"You wouldn't after a week."

I laughed, remembering how I felt right after boot camp. "Maybe."

I studied the small Arab village that was nestled at the foot of the hill where we parked. Arab villages were always distinct from Israeli settlements because of the way the Arabs built their houses—gray cubes of unpainted cinderblocks with square windows placed haphazardly throughout. Some villages were friendly to Jews and sold food or pottery. There was one that my parents used to go to for soft white cheese and locally pressed olive oil. But there was always a mild sense of danger involved. You might arrive right after some mullah announced death to all Jews again. The dust-colored houses looked neglected even from a distance. I didn't see anyone out in the streets.

Dov handed me a bottle of water and I drank. The sky was perfectly blue, and there was a mild breeze that carried the smell of rosemary. I rarely got the chance to be in the countryside. Once again, I was struck by how beautiful and peaceful it was. I felt Dov watching me.

"What?" I brushed at my hair self-consciously.

"You've got some crumbs on your face." He leaned in and touched my cheek. I stayed very still. My heart was racing. I didn't know what to do with my hands. Please, I thought. But I didn't know what I wanted. For him to kiss me, maybe. For me to be cool, definitely. To be a good kisser.

He brushed a finger across my lips and gently tucked a strand of my hair behind my ear.

"You're so beautiful," he said. His words brushed by my ear and I closed my eyes. His lips brushed mine. I leaned forward a little. To let him know.

He settled into the kiss and I relaxed with a sigh.

This is perfect, I thought. Just perfect.

He cradled my face between his hands, kissing me, and the bottle of water I held slipped out of my fingers and fell to the ground. His lips were soft against mine. I reached up and touched his face.

"Hey, Israeli fuckers!"

We scrambled apart. Dov jumped up and stood in front of me. I looked all around me until I spotted them. Three ragged little boys, wearing cut-off jeans and dusty shirts. They were twenty meters away. I stood up, trying to see around Dov.

"Did you come to fuck each other in front of our village?" one of them shouted.

My mouth gaped open for a moment. It was almost funny to hear a tiny voice saying such things. He couldn't have been more than eight. There was nothing here for Dov to fight.

"Go away, Jewish whore," another one shouted.

I wanted to tell them they'd been watching too much television. I wanted to ask if their parents knew where they were.

Then the third one bent down, picked up a stone, and hurled it our way. It fell short.

"I'm going to kill those little bastards," Dov said. He started heading their way. The boys scrambled back. One of them picked up a glass bottle and threw it at us too. It landed on a rock and exploded into shards of flying glass. I looked down at my leg and saw I'd been nicked. A small trail of blood started trickling down my leg.

"Let's get out of here," I said.

Dov looked at them and I could see he wanted to go over and beat the crap out of them. His hands were clenched at his sides and his shoulders were hunched.

"No," I said, trying to control my voice, grabbing awkwardly for his arm. "Don't! Just get us out of here." My legs were shaking and I felt panic edging in. I was bleeding. Headlines and news briefs were flashing through my mind. This is how tragedies happen, I kept thinking. We could easily become the evening news if this escalated any further. "They're just stupid kids. Don't let them think they mean anything."

"I'm not running away from some snot-nosed kids."

When they saw that I'd stopped Dov, they edged closer again, their jeers growing louder and their throws getting closer and closer to the jeep. One landed on the hood with a loud "ping" and I could see the dent and scratch it made.

"Dov!" I shook him. "Let's go!"

This wasn't some prank that naughty boys play. They hated us. They were eight, and I was scared of them the way I would be of a pack of wild dogs.

"You want those little assholes to get away with this?"

"You don't know who's out there," I pleaded. "Their dad or uncle could be nearby with a rifle. Please—" my voice cracked. "Let's leave!"

With a disgusted look at them, he turned around.

They cheered.

Dov started the jeep, gunned it, and we took off, leaving the boys, the remains of our lunch, and the field where we'd just had our first real kiss, in a brown cloud of dust and hate.

Chapter Seven

VIRGINIA

I woke up to the sound of my dog, Kipi, scratching at the door to come in. I groaned and sat up to let her in, but as soon as I opened my eyes, I realized it was only Payton gathering her papers for her eight o'clock class.

"Sorry," she whispered. "I was trying to be quiet. I'll be out of here in two more seconds."

"'S okay," I mumbled, and rolled over, burrowing under the covers. My new flannel sheets were warm, and I rubbed my cheek on my pillow. I'd say that much for living in a cold climate—which is what Virginia had become in the last few weeks—it made snuggling in bed even more of a joy. It had been so brutally cold last night at the astronomy observatory. A sudden cold so crisp I thought even the stars would shatter. A preview of what winter must be like here. "Unseasonable chill," the weatherman called it, and I shuddered to think what it'd be like when it was seasonable for such cold. I was warm now and I planned to stay that way. I wiggled my toes, happy that they seemed to have survived the night intact.

The door clicked shut behind Payton.

It was too bad I couldn't bring Kipi here, right now—her little body would fit perfectly in the space by my belly. She'd sprawl on her back with her legs spread and I'd scratch her stomach and play with her ears. But university dorms didn't let you keep dogs, and even if they did, I couldn't have brought her with me. The flight alone would have traumatized her.

What would she think of the cold? I pictured her playing in the snow Payton kept promising would come. I imagined her jumping into a snowy drift and disappearing with a poof of white flakes.

I must have fallen asleep because I nearly fell out of bed when the phone rang.

"Maya, did I wake you? Your mother said the morning was the best time to call . . . and it's almost nine in the morning, right? Or did I get it wrong?"

"Hen," I said groggily. My eyes were weighted with anvils. I forced them open. My voice sounded like I had a two-pack habit, as smooth as sandpaper. "Yeah, it's almost nine. I should be up by now." A lie, since I was planning to skip class and sleep until ten-thirty. But no matter.

I had meant to call Hen before now. I never felt up to it, never had the energy for mental fencing. She produced guilt as a defensive secretion, like a skunk. So now I tried to wake up my fuzzy brain, to make sure I said the right thing.

"So how is school? Do you have any friends yet?"

"Hen," I protested. "What kind of question is that? Of course I have friends. People here are terrific." I was mildly surprised to discover as I said it that it was true.

"And are you eating? Can you find any food besides hamburgers?" Hen was not a vegetarian but was still convinced any weight gain came directly from eating meat. Weight gain was a favorite topic of hers. She could make a POW feel uneasy about his daily caloric intake.

"There's a salad bar in the cafeteria," I said. "I eat a salad every day."

"You shouldn't use a cream-based dressing, it's just a sneaky way of saying oil and butter. It defeats the whole point of eating a salad."

"Of course."

"Americans don't know how to eat."

Annoyed, I felt I had to defend American cuisine. "That's not true, Hen. It's not as bad as people think. There's lots of good food." I tried to think of compelling examples. "The sandwiches here are wonderful, they have good pasta. Even the salad bar is pretty good."

"But not like in Israel."

"No." I was forced to agree. "There's nothing like the food in Israel." I sighed, thinking about it. "I miss tomatoes the most. The ones here are almost pink. They have no taste. There's no hummus, no good olives." Didn't I mean to defend American food? Hen always got me to agree with her in the end.

"I miss having you here in my apartment," she said, as if thinking the same thing.

"Yeah," I said. "It's very different here."

"That'll make it easier for you to come back." I could hear the satisfied smile over six thousand miles of telephone cables, or whatever they use these days.

"I got another award yesterday," she said. "A glass pyramid they pretended was crystal." Hen was the only person I knew who could tell the difference between glass and crystal. Until I met her I didn't even know there was a difference. "I don't know where they expect me to store all this nonsense they keep handing out."

"What did you get it for?"

"I don't remember," she said. "They give them out too easily. Close a deal, organize a function, blow your nose, and *voilà*, another glass pyramid to dust."

I laughed. "Hen, you are one of a kind." I thought again how amusing it was that in Hebrew Hen's name meant charm and beauty, while in English it was the word for a female chicken.

"I know. Anyway, I was just calling to check on you for your mother. Make sure that you were still alive." I knew that wasn't true, but it was so like Hen to need an excuse to call me. To blame my silly mother for worrying.

"You're a good sister for doing that," I said. "Tell her everything is fine. Tell her I'm doing well."

"And sleeping in until noon," Hen said. "Obviously someone is having a good time. Just don't do anything I wouldn't do."

I gently hung up the phone and sat in bed, blanket around my shoulders like an Indian chief, thinking.

It was a perfectly beautiful day, not too hot or too cold, with an easy, steady breeze that made me want to sigh in pleasure. Restless and feeling like I was wasting a precious day in the cool, dark library, I gathered up my books and notes, jammed them in my bag, and walked out into the sunshine. Students were stretched out on the grass or playing Frisbee. I found an unoccupied bench nearby and sat down.

I exhaled deeply, feeling the sun warm my skin. I suspected I wouldn't get too many perfect days before it got cold. So I sat on the bench and ignored the piles of books I should have been reviewing, ignored the students around me, closed my eyes, and lounged like a lizard, letting the sun warm my limbs.

I opened my eyes a moment later when a dark shadow spilled over me and cut off the heat and light like a switch.

"Sunbathing, Greenland?"

I squinted at the figure blocking the sun and recognized Justin.

"Move over," I said. "Or sit down, but don't block the sun."

He sat down next to me and stretched out his long legs. It had been almost a month since the kissing incident, and neither he nor I had brought it up or even alluded to it in any way. This was the first time I had seen him outside class since then. He glanced over at me, then slouched down so his head could rest against the back of the bench, like mine. He tilted his head back, sighed, and closed his eyes. When I saw that he seemed content to stay put, I turned my face back to the sun and closed my eyes.

We stayed silent like that for a while and it was very peaceful.

"Nice, isn't it?" I finally said.

"Yeah. Been a while since I did this."

"Me too." He left a comfortable distance between us, but I was still very aware of him, his body so close to me. "We should have discussion outside on days like this."

"I tried it before," he said, his eyes still closed. "No one pays attention."

"No one pays attention anyway."

It wasn't true. Most days the discussions were actually interesting. Justin could point to connections and consequences that I never saw on my own. I even found myself reading sources not on the reading list just so I'd have something meaningful and surprising to add.

"You've read Thurgood Marshall's decision on this?" he asked the first time I quoted something different.

"It seemed relevant," I shrugged, secretly pleased by his tone.

Now on the bench, he just laughed.

"They teach you how to be cruel in Greenland, or does it just come naturally for you?"

"That wasn't cruel," I said, smiling. "You haven't seen cruel. And I'm from Israel, you know. I can't believe you still think I'm from Greenland."

I had meant to tell him that for weeks. He seemed to enjoy bringing up Greenland every time we met. It was past time to set him straight. I just didn't want to do it in front of fifteen other students. I wasn't as paranoid about letting people know where I was from, but I didn't want to make a production of it. I didn't know what I was afraid of—maybe that people would sneer or make assumptions. Would he call me Israel now? Somehow I didn't think so.

"I hadn't guessed that," he said. He opened his eyes and turned to look at me. "I thought maybe Italy or Argentina. I hadn't thought Israel."

"Now you know." He'd thought about me. I was pleased. I was also impressed that he had never asked me.

"So what do you think of our fair country?" he asked.

I was going to give him a flippant answer, but his tone was serious and the sun had worked out the kinks in my neck and the tension from my body.

"It's peaceful here," I said. "I hadn't even known what the word meant until I came here." I took a deep breath, held it, and then let it out. "It feels like nothing bad could ever happen here."

And then we were both quiet again.

When Payton noticed me and came over a few minutes later, I introduced her to Justin. From the flare of interest in her eye and the significant looks she kept shooting me, I knew that even if I tried to tell her he was just my TA and not a love interest, she'd never believe me.

I met Chris again that evening in front of the cafeteria. Our running styles fit well together, and we kept up our twice-a-week runs. We were both slow and steady, preferring time and distance to speed. I suspected Chris could have run faster, but he wasn't complaining and I liked having a running partner.

As we ran, he grumbled about his girlfriend, Tasha. She worked at a bank back in Blacksburg and was very close to her mother. He talked about her every once in a while, usually when he'd just gotten off the phone with her.

"I would love to get stationed in Japan," Chris told me, his breath coming even and steady. "I went there two years ago and it was awesome. Totally different. I could have spent years there and I still wouldn't have seen anything." It always surprised me when Chris mentioned travel or sophisticated interests. There was something very humble and unpretentious about him, and he looked exactly like a dumb marine who should only be capable of shouting out "Yes, sir!" or "No, sir!" When he talked about attending a tea ceremony or going to a Turkish bathhouse, it always threw me.

"Tasha just doesn't see it," he said, eyes straight ahead, head up, perfect running form. "We've talked about getting married, but she said she'd never move to Japan. Too far away from her mother, can you believe it?" He shook his head and glanced down at me. "I'm in the Marine Corps. There're no bases in Blacksburg. I don't know what she's thinking."

I looked at him out of the corner of my eye and then concentrated on opening up my stride. He had sped up as he talked. I waited until I could feel that pause between each step, when both legs were far apart, striding out, and I floated for a split second, legs scissoring like pendulums.

As I opened my step, I sped up just past Chris. He increased his pace almost unconsciously, keeping even with me, his breath still coming nice and easy, his running form still perfect. I realized how much faster he could run and I wondered why he kept calling me to jog with him.

"She says I'm more committed to the Marine Corps than I am to her. What's that supposed to mean?"

I took it as a rhetorical question. We ran for a while in silence. I focused on keeping my breath steady, since I was running faster than usual. The trees and streetlights were flashing by, there and gone, and I was a force of nature. Unstoppable.

"It's not about her," he finally said. "It's not a choice between her and the Marine Corps. It's about whether she wants safety or adventure in her life."

It seemed to me that Tasha actually understood things pretty well. If it was about whether she wanted to join him and the military or whether she wanted to stay home without him, if those were her only two choices, that meant the Marine Corps did come first to Chris.

"We've dated since high school, and she's never left our hometown. She went to the community college there, still lives five minutes away from her folks. I'm not saying there's anything wrong with that, but if you have a chance to explore, how can you turn it down?"

It was the most he'd said about himself or Tasha since we'd started running together.

"I don't know," I said. "Some people aren't like that. Some people find what they like and they're happy to stay there."

"You make it sound like a good thing."

We exchanged looks, because it was clear neither one of us was like that. I was here in the States instead of home in Israel, and he couldn't wait to cross an ocean.

Poor Tasha was about to be dumped for the open road and the brotherhood of the Marine Corps. There it was again, personality, force of will, leaving you where you started or moving you along.

"We'd come back," he said. "I told her that I plan to live in Blacksburg again one day. She'd be away from her mother for a few years, big deal. Everything would still be the same when we'd get back."

Maybe Tasha had the right idea. If you knew that you were happy someplace, it was a good thing to stay put. I missed the hot beat of Middle Eastern music that always blared from the radio. I missed hanging out with my friends and not having to think about what comes out of my mouth. I missed my family. I fought the urge to glance at my watch. I dropped my arms, shook them to relax them, and thought about my breathing. In, out. Like a heartbeat. Slow and steady.

When we finished, we stretched on the grass.

"Go easy on her," I said, propping my ankle on the bike stand and stretching my hamstring. "Be patient. She might change her mind."

"I know," he said, grunting as he imitated my stretch. "But even if she went, we'd both know I dragged her there and that she'd rather be home, eating at the Golden Corral. We just don't want the same things."

"No, I guess you don't."

Dov and I wanted the same things. We just didn't know how to get there. He had finished his military service seven months before I did, and he'd gone to work for his uncle's computer company, writing software. He still lived with his parents. Even with Hen's casual attitude and long workdays, it felt wrong for me to bring Dov over to her place and do anything more than kiss. I always worried she'd pop in, needing to grab some files from her home office. At his place, I could hear his mother watching television in the next room. Even though he swore she'd never walk in on us when the door was closed, I couldn't relax and I wouldn't let him take off my shirt. It drove him crazy.

"She won't care," he said, nearly grinding his teeth. "She already thinks we have sex. So why not do it?"

We'd been going out for nine months. We made love for the first time four months earlier. We made love again a month after that. But opportunities were few and far between, and we'd fought over this ever since the first time we slept together at his cousin's place. As far as Dov was concerned, after that first time the floodgates were opened, so to speak, and we should be making love on a regular basis.

"I can't," I said. "I just don't feel right."

We hardly ever had any privacy. I had a cousin who'd lend us her place when she was away, and there was Dov's cousin, who had a place. But if they were in town, then—as far as I was concerned—Dov was out of luck.

One Friday night, we'd both drunk more than usual and Dov's frustration with me had mounted. His fevered brain was plotting, though I didn't know it. It was three in the morning and we'd stumbled out of a club near the beach. We were in

Haifa for once, visiting my parents. We'd had dinner with them and then Dov and I went out.

"I've had too much to drink," he said, taking a deep breath of the salty air. "I shouldn't drive."

My ears were ringing slightly from the music in the club and the air around me seemed soothing and quiet. I didn't want to go home yet. "So let's walk."

The club was right on the shore, so we took off our shoes and walked to the water's edge. After a while, Dov said he was tired. He put his arm around me and rested his cheek on my hair. I thought I felt him kiss my hairline, but it was so soft I couldn't be sure. We found a dry sand dune and sat down. We looked at the stars for a bit, but there wasn't much to see; the city lights washed away most of the stars.

He leaned over and kissed me. My heart thumped pleasantly as it always did when I felt those firm warm lips and his hand cupped the back of my head. I was buzzed pretty good, and soon his clever hands were under my shirt, plucking at my bra.

"Wait," I mumbled, feeling half-drugged. "There're people around."

I could faintly hear people laughing. An open-air bar not far from us was doing brisk business, and people sat on the sand drinking beer.

"Who cares," Dov said, his voice rumbling in my ear. My hands tightened involuntary on his shirt. He kissed my ear, bit lightly on my earlobe. "Even if they notice, they'll just see two people making out on the beach. Happens all the time." He rained tiny kisses on my face, the line of my jaw, my neck, and then returned to my lips, kissing me deeply, making love to my mouth.

I barely heard him. The ringing in my ears had grown.

"Okay," I whispered as his hand slipped under the waistband of my pants. "Yes."

I showered after we crept back home. I studied myself in the bathroom mirror, satisfied little smirk and all. My hair was a tangled mess, full of sand and salt from the damp wind. The sand had gotten everywhere, and Dov, with a grin, asked if I needed any help getting it out.

"No," I said, and kicked him out of the bathroom.

I was embarrassed but also slightly proud. Sex on the beach. Not bad for a nice girl from Haifa. Next thing, I'd join the mile-high club.

I still had energy after the run with Chris, so I walked to the gym and worked out in the weight room for forty minutes. I wanted my muscles to quiver with fatigue. I wanted to push out all the memories, sweat them right out of my skin.

I passed Brook Maxwell, ex-flame of Justin Case. She was wearing black spandex tights and a lilac sports bra, climbing and climbing on the Stairmaster but getting nowhere. I was wearing ratty sweatpants and a faded shirt, stained dark with sweat. Her eyes shifted from the fashion magazine in front of her to me and then shifted back without acknowledgment. I flicked her the middle finger but she didn't see.

* * *

For the next two weeks, Payton was consumed by sorority rush. Eight hours a day in her high heels and making conversation with perfect strangers was trying even for Payton. I was surprised how disappointed I was when I'd find our room empty at the end of the day. We hardly met for dinner anymore, and when I did see her during the day, she was too busy to say more than a quick hello, always surrounded by her group of fellow rushees. Like a string of little Goldilockses, they went from sorority house to sorority house trying to find the perfect fit. I'd never seen Payton fuss so much with her hair, her makeup, or her clothes.

I shrugged to myself in the empty room, quiet after Payton's frantic search for a hair clip and her quick good-bye. I was thinking that it shouldn't matter that we never did anything together anymore. But it did.

Two weeks later, Payton was accepted into the sorority of her choice and was giddy with the knowledge that another Walker woman would be a Kappa Delta. Having passed from prospective rushee to first-year pledge, Payton was consumed with secret rituals, Big Sister Week, and elaborate functions. I was constantly taking down messages, accepting little gifts—plastic cups full of candy decorated with Greek letters, framed photos of Kappa Deltas having fun, T-shirts with the sorority's Greek letters—and leaving them on her bed, like offerings for a benevolent goddess.

Payton would be out until past midnight on weeknights and not back until dawn on the weekends. She started skipping her morning classes, unable to get up before ten.

"I don't know how much more I can take," she croaked to

me one night. "They say in a week things'll settle down, but I'm behind in all my classes. God, I'm so tired." She flopped into bed and was asleep with all her clothes on by the time I turned out the lights.

Then the onslaught was over and we were back to having dinner together two or three nights a week.

Payton's mother took us out to their country club to celebrate her daughter's brilliant success.

We lunched on chicken salad on croissants, fruit salad, and sweet iced tea. Several women wearing Chanel suits in pastel colors stopped by our table to say hello. Payton and I pasted on polite smiles that stayed in place for nearly an hour.

Her mother was very chatty and hardly let Payton get a word in, waving gladly anytime someone she knew walked by. She'd ask a question and not give Payton a chance to answer. After being cut off mid-sentence for the fourth or fifth time, Payton caught the look I shot her and grimaced.

While the plates were cleared away, both Payton and I excused ourselves to the restroom.

"She's my mom," Payton said before I could say anything, sadness and frustration warring in her tone. "That's just who she is."

"Is it her medication?" I knew I probably wasn't supposed to ask, but I did.

"I don't know. It might be. Sometimes she just gets this way." Payton entered a stall and closed the door. I leaned against the counter, waiting for her to finish, trying to think of something to say.

Payton came out and briskly washed her hands.

"The desserts here are unbelievable. Have you ever had pecan pie?"

I admitted that I had not.

"Then today is your lucky day," Payton said. "They have the most amazing pecan pie here."

I understood that she didn't want to talk about it anymore.

After her mother dropped us off in her dark-green Jaguar, Payton plopped on her bed. "I hope the club wasn't too rough for you," she said, pretending that was why we were both slightly subdued. "But my family pretty much has to go there. My great-grandfather helped found the club."

I followed her lead.

"Tough," I nodded sympathetically.

"You know what I mean." She threw her pillow at me.

I ducked and it hit my shoulder.

"It must be hard," I said. "Going to a fancy club, day after day, pecan after pecan."

"We try to be brave about it."

"Yes, I can see that."

She laughed. "Now that you've mocked my family and our proud heritage, are you going to help me with this calculus nonsense?"

"Calculus is many things," I sniffed. "But nonsense isn't one of them." I scooted over to her bed, and we spread out her notes and worked on figuring out proofs, theorems, and the value of the unknown.

* * *

That afternoon I met the major's Israeli wife, Yael, for coffee. She lived in a nice house not far from the university. The directions she gave me over the phone were impeccable, and I found the house ten minutes before I was supposed to arrive. I strolled down her street, admiring the different houses with their long windows and lush gardens until it was time, and then I rang the bell.

A slim blond woman wearing blue cotton pants and a snug white shirt opened the door.

"Maya," she said warmly in English. "Come in. You found the place okay?"

"Perfectly."

"I've been looking forward to meeting you."

The house was decorated in a strange mix of Israeli and American styles. There were several prints of Jerusalem, an embroidered blessing of the house in Hebrew—clearly her contributions. The tan recliner in front of the television and the military prints of historic uniforms must have belonged to her American husband.

She had set out plates with cookies and fruit, and a little pitcher of cream and sugar in a matching silver set. I was officially a Real Guest.

We settled down, poured ourselves a cup of coffee, and added the necessary adjustments of cream and sugar. I helped myself to a cookie, knowing nothing would get said until I did so.

"We can talk in Hebrew, right?" she asked me. Her accent in English was very soft, nothing like the harsh tones most people in Israel carry when speaking English.

"Of course," I said. "I've been looking forward to speaking Hebrew again. Apart from my parents on the phone, I never get to speak it."

She nodded sympathetically.

"I only speak Hebrew with my mother and sister these days," she said, switching to Hebrew. "I tried to teach my kids Hebrew—I've got a son and a daughter—but it's too hard." She shrugged. "They didn't want to learn it as kids. Their father doesn't speak it and their friends don't speak it and they thought it was embarrassing that their mother did. Now they're grown up and they want to know why I never taught it to them." She gave a little laugh and sipped her coffee.

"Does your family in Israel speak English?" I asked.

"Some, but not well."

"That's hard. I mean, they're your family but they can hardly communicate with your kids."

Yael waved away my concern. "They can understand the important things. Besides, seventy percent of communication is body language. When you have that and you love each other, you understand just about everything."

I blinked at her blithe explanation. It sounded like she must say it a lot. I had this vivid mental image of little kids pantomiming licking an ice cream and their grandmother pantomiming back looking for her wallet and keys. I was sure my professors would be interested to know that the grammar mistakes I made in my papers weren't important and were irrelevant to getting my point across.

"That's . . . good." At least my parents spoke Hebrew and

English well. No matter where I chose to live and have kids, they'd be able to talk with them using more than just hand signs and foot taps. It was something I'd already thought about if I stayed here.

"You make a place for yourself, no matter where you end up," she said, as if reading my mind. I had to be careful not to let my thoughts show on my face. "I never imagined myself as an American, living all over the world on military bases. But that's how things worked out, and now I can't imagine it any other way."

"It must have been hard."

She shrugged and made a face.

"I can see that being here now might be hard for you. But it's hard for me when I go back to Israel now. I'm not fully Israeli anymore. I know I'm not really American either. But you learn not to define yourself that way."

I was taken aback and didn't have an easy comment to return. I suddenly realized that I'd found a person who might help me figure out what to do, how to make the choice of picking my country, my homeland. The afternoon switched from being a tedious chore to being something that might truly help me.

"Okay," I said, scooting forward in my seat, carefully setting down my cup. "How does this work? How do you learn to be comfortable here? Or do you?"

She put down her mug as well. We had both figuratively rolled up our sleeves. "You have to choose," she said softly. "You need to decide what team you play for. I'm not saying you need to do it now; you don't know yet. But give it two years and then decide one way or the other. And this doesn't mean there aren't days when you're homesick. And it doesn't mean you don't pay close attention to the news every time they mention Israel. You're still connected. But in your heart, you need to decide that if push came to shove, whose side you're on, and then stay there. Don't second-guess yourself."

I must have looked uneasy because she smiled. "Don't worry about it so much. I think in the end it's not a decision your head makes. It's an instinct you develop. A gut feeling that you follow. It doesn't signify love or a lack of it—" she stopped herself, thought for a moment. "You'll know when you decide because you'll talk about something and you'll say 'we' about one country and 'they' about the other country. I know right now you think that the only people who love you are in Israel, right?"

I nodded.

"And that no one can love you like that here. So how can you leave the people who love you so much, who understand who you are. Am I right?"

I nodded.

"Well, here's my story. I met my husband when he was stationed in Israel. We started dating and we got married three months later."

"Wow."

She smiled. "It makes sense when you're nineteen, let me tell you. Anyway, the first year we were married he was still stationed in Israel, so things were really easy. Ian's not Jewish, but he didn't care about religion. We went to my parents' house for the holiday. Ian wore a *kipa*. I had everything the way I was used to it. But after a year, we got assigned to this place called Parris Island, which has nothing to do with Paris, France. And I'm not talking some nice fun island. It's the headquarters for Marine Corps recruiting. I'm talking about mosquitoes and some godforsaken swamps in the middle of nowhere." She paused, took a sip of her drink, smiled as I winced in sympathy. "Two days before we're supposed to leave Israel for South Carolina, Ian gets a three-month assignment to Haiti that he can't talk about. On his way out the door he tells me there's no housing available for us in Parris Island but that some chaplain priest, hearing about our plight, has agreed to share his house with us." She was a good storyteller, pausing at the right places, building up her tale.

"Are you serious?"

"Yeah. I nearly had a nervous breakdown."

"Why didn't you just stay in Israel until he came back?"

"Well, I said I wouldn't go. I said he couldn't abandon me and send me to a priest's house. Apart from one trip to visit his family in Michigan, I'd never spent time in the States. I'd never met a priest."

I nodded my head. I'd never met a priest either.

"But," she lifted a finger. "I was six months pregnant, and the one thing Ian asked of me when we got married is that the kids be born in the States. He didn't care if I raised them Jewish, he didn't care if I kept a kosher house, but he wanted the kids born on American soil. So I went."

"Unbelievable." I shook my head. "That's incredible."

She smiled. "I ranted and raved for two hours and then my parents drove us to the airport. I got on one plane, he got on another." She set down her cup, clearly enjoying my reactions to her story. "I flew by myself—another first—with my belly already out to here." She held a hand two feet away from her stomach. "When I landed, the priest was waiting for me with my name on a sign. I was so upset to be in this new country, I nearly cried when I saw him. I'd been wondering what I would do if I landed and there was no one waiting for me. I was ready to throw myself into his arms.

"I grew up in a religious home. We kept kosher and my father went to synagogue every morning. And here I was, going to live with a man who wasn't my husband, alone in his house, and he was a priest. It nearly killed me. I didn't even tell my parents, I was so ashamed and worried about their reaction."

"They were okay with the fact that you didn't marry a Jew?"

"No." She shook her head. "Not at all, but for once in my life I didn't care what they thought. Sometimes you only listen to yourself, and my parents realized they couldn't change my mind. They could keep me as their daughter who married a goy, or they could lose a daughter who married a goy." She shrugged. "They decided to keep me."

"Wow."

"Wait until you fall in love," she said. "The strangest things can happen."

It took a physical effort for me not to flinch at the blow. I swallowed back the rush of memories that suddenly crowded the edge of my mind and forced myself to focus on the rest of her story.

"By the time we arrived at the priest's house, I was nearly shaking. He showed me where he'd put up a mezuzah on the doorframe. He showed me the kitchen. He had turned it into a kosher kitchen. He'd gone out and bought two sets of dishes, forks, spoons, everything you need. He had taken down all the crucifixes from the walls. Then he took me to one small bedroom and he said, 'This is my bedroom.' There was a bed and a dresser and a crucifix over the bed. That was the only place in the whole house with one. Then he showed me the master bedroom. 'This is where you're going to sleep.' It was a beautiful room. 'This is your house now,' he said. 'I won't be in your way.' "

Goose bumps raced up my arms. "He really put up a mezuzah and koshered the kitchen?"

"He did. He got some man from a synagogue in Savannah to come in and help him do it right. I started crying, and he got very worried. This was twenty years ago and everyone thought it wasn't healthy for a pregnant woman to be upset. So he starts saying, 'Did I do something wrong? I'm sorry, it'll be fixed, please don't worry. We can make it right.' Then I started crying even harder because he had done everything perfectly, so thoughtfully. I'd expected him to try to convert me, and instead he gave up his house to Judaism." I noticed her eyes had welled up. She looked away. "Even today I can't get over it. We became very good friends. When David was born, he was there with Ian in the hospital waiting room."

I sipped my coffee. It was almost cold and tasted like wood.

"Maya, what I'm trying to tell you is that no matter where you end up making your home, people make room for you. People who you never thought would accept you. You don't have to hide who you are or try to conform." She looked at me sharply, as if she could see my walls. "You couldn't blend in even if you tried. So you shouldn't bother."

I thanked her for the coffee and said it was time for me to go. We shook hands.

"You'll have to come here for Rosh Hashanah," she said.

On my way out the door I turned and asked her, "Are you still friends, you and the priest?"

She looked down for a moment. "No," she said. "We kept in touch for almost ten years, and then he got out of the military and we lost touch."

I said good-bye and walked away.

I didn't want to think about Yael or her hybrid house or her American husband and their nomadic military existence. So I walked through the quiet neighborhood, taking the long way back to the library, trying to keep my mind clear. But I couldn't help thinking about friendships and respect and making space in your life for people different than you are. As always when I met someone new, I wondered if Dov would have liked her. I tried to remember if I thought about him this much when he was alive, but by now it was all tied up together and I couldn't remember. It seemed like there was never a time when he wasn't in my thoughts.

I forced myself to focus on my breath, lungs filling in and emptying, oxygen-rich blood reaching all the nooks and crannies of my body. Call it Zen walking. Zen avoidance. Meditative denial.

In this state of false Eastern calm, I ran into Justin and Brook, the two people I knew who seemed to absolutely fit together, like yachts and Kennebunkport. I didn't want to be seen and I didn't want to chat. I was seriously eyeing the giant SUV on my right as an excellent hiding place, but I was spotted before I could dive behind its monster fenders. As always, I hesitated on my instincts and waited too long.

"Hey, Maya. What are you up to?" Justin sounded happy to see me, oblivious to the fact that Brook and I had our hackles raised. I couldn't really articulate what it was between her and me. Maybe it was that she seemed perfect and all-American and still wasn't happy. I couldn't stand to see someone so spoiled that she could be unhappy with an easy, beautiful life. I wasn't sure why she didn't like me either. I don't know if she thought I was a rival or if she was naturally hostile to other women. But it was clear that neither one of us was happy to see the other.

"Hey, Justin," I said. "Hi, Brook."

She gave me a closed smile and a slight inclination of the head. I debated between curtsying or giving her the finger, but restrained myself.

"We're off for a cup of coffee on the Corner, want to join us?" Justin asked.

I considered accepting for the joy of tormenting Brook, but

then was tempted to say no to spare myself an hour of hostilities. And then I remembered what Yael said and decided, evilly, to put it to the test.

"Are you sure there's room for me?" I asked. "I'd hate to intrude."

"Not at all," Justin said, and Brook, who maybe hesitated on her instincts too, missed her chance. "We'd love for you to come."

So we went, the three of us, and I had my fourth cup of coffee of the day.

Playing with the brown packets of natural sugar, regretting the impulse that landed me here, I listened to Justin explain their mission on Rugby Road.

"The houses on Rugby Road are, architecturally, some of the most interesting homes in Charlottesville," he began. "That big sunken field across from the Bayly Art Museum was where the slaves and laborers dug the red clay to make the bricks that built the university."

I sipped my cappuccino and listened to him ramble. It was actually interesting at times, since I jogged along Rugby Road and knew the buildings he was talking about. I would never have guessed the history that had occurred behind those staid Colonial walls.

Brook laid a possessive hand on Justin's arm as he talked, but he kept gesturing with his arms and her hand would get knocked off. It was kind of entertaining to watch this keep happening. I wondered if they even noticed. It seemed very appropriate. Maybe I should study psychology instead of astronomy, I thought.

I finished my coffee. I could feel it twanging through my system, and it was hard to keep my hands still.

Justin finished describing his latest interview with a former resident who had lived on Rugby during the twenties.

"You found her coherent?" I asked. "She must be past ninety."

"Next spring, yeah. She invited me to her birthday party."

"Isn't that sweet," I said. "She likes you."

"Women of all ages have a hard time resisting my charms," he said. He nudged Brook with his shoulder and she managed a smile.

"See?"

"Yeah," I said. "Really charming."

"Speaking of charming," he said, rising from his seat. "Excuse me, ladies, the coffee runneth through me."

"Even more charming," I said. Justin seemed to bring out my old sarcasm.

He gave a small bow and headed to the back of the café, leaving Brook and me to stare at each other across the small table.

Neither of us had anything left in our cups, so we couldn't pretend to be busy with those. I rested my elbows on the table and tried to think about what I needed to do that afternoon. I tried not to think of Yael and her theories. I tried not to think about Hen back home, working hard, living it up. About Chris and his girlfriend, about Justin and what I may or may not have been feeling for him.

Brook shifted in her seat. I wanted to smile. I wasn't bothered by silence at the table, but I guess in her book this was an uncomfortable thing.

She huffed, shifted again, and looked over her shoulder at the back of the café to see if Justin was coming. He wasn't.

"Justin and I have known each other since high school."

"That's nice."

She glared at me. "We grew up in the same neighborhood."

"How interesting," I drawled.

"I just thought you should know. Since you seemed," she paused, "interested in him."

I narrowed my eyes.

"Look, it's obvious you have some kind of crush on your TA," she said, her voice like nails on a chalkboard. "Everyone goes through that, but you need to know that Justin is a big flirt and he can be careless of people's feelings."

"Like yours?"

She stiffened. Her nostrils flared as if she'd just smelled something foul.

"I know you're from Israel and that things are different there." I noted a shift in her tone of voice. "But here in America, you don't just take what you want when you want it. Helpless Palestinian refugees might let you get away with that, but not here."

Okay. That just made things easy. Instead of telling her I had no interest in her ex-boyfriend, instead of reassuring her that he was all hers to stalk as she pleased, I lost it.

"You don't have a bloody clue." My wired tongue tripped

and fell over the words. I was sick with doubts and suppressed anger, with all that caffeine racing through my system, and my heart was beating too fast. I stood and my chair scraped back loudly. People turned to look. Brook had a smug look on her face. She wanted this. But I didn't care.

"I was wondering if you could possibly be as stupid as you look," I said, and to my ears, my voice was low and harsh. The American pronunciations I'd worked on were gone. "You're perfectly stupid. I wasn't your enemy and I don't have a crush on your idiotic former boyfriend. Who, by the way, wants nothing to do with you. But now that you've insulted me and my country, I'll take him away from you just for spite. And you'll be able to do nothing about it, you fucking anti-Semite." I held on to my bag with both hands. I was shaking. So was she.

The few people sitting nearby were staring at me with their mouths literally hanging open. I saw Justin coming out of the bathroom, heading back to our table. He saw me and looked surprised that I was standing, that I was leaving. I hurried out of the café before he could reach me. Let that little bitch tell him whatever she wanted. I hardly cared.

I walked, head down, watching my feet, still hugging my schoolbag to my chest.

I wanted to laugh or scream or slam my fist into a wall. Fuck 'em, I thought, picking up the pace. Yael living half a life like a bird in love with a fish. Stupid Brook playing out of her league trying to protect her worthless ex-boyfriend from his wandering eye. And brainless, beautiful Justin who spends his time researching the life of buildings and the youth of old women, too blind to see what's right in front of him, deluding himself about friendships. I kicked a stone and watched with satisfaction as it hurled away, slamming into a tree and pinging off at a crazy angle. They weren't worth my time. Let Brook lose sleep dreaming up images of me seducing Justin. I wanted nothing more to do with them. Maybe finding my place would be easy. This country was populated entirely by aliens.

Chapter Eight

ISRAEL

I drove with Hen to the airport to pick up François Levieux, a consultant from Paris looking to inspect Israeli companies for future investments. Hen's firm had picked her as the welcoming committee because she was fluent in English. And I, speaking a little French and decent English, was convinced and bribed by Hen (bribed quite well this time) to come along. Levieux would spend a week in Israel, touring various facilities and meeting vice presidents and the CEOs, but for today it was only Hen and me.

"Looks better to have two beautiful women meet him at the airport than just one. The French admire beauty and aesthetics," she said. As far as I knew, Hen had been to France only once, on a four-day trip to Paris, so I didn't know where this intimate knowledge of the French psyche was coming from. But who was I to argue? It got me out of work for the day. It was frightening sometimes the strings that Hen could pull.

We got all dressed up. Hen wore a periwinkle silk suit with a thigh-high slit that showed the lace top of her hose as she walked. I wore trophies of my increased skill as an extortionist: a black pantsuit with round lapels, like a dress from the fifties, and no shirt underneath. Sometimes I suspected Hen dressed me as an accessory to her outfits. There was no denying that we turned a lot of heads on our way from the car to the terminal. I wondered if part of the plan was for Hen to seduce unsuspecting, aesthetics-loving François.

Hen held a discreet sign with his name, and we stood slightly apart from the families crowding the fence around International Arrivals.

People were already pouring out, pushing carts piled high with suitcases and bags. I carefully looked at each man coming out, trying to guess which one was our French consultant. Several handsome men in smooth suits eyed our sign, but they kept going.

A slim woman with greasy hair and ice-blue eyes like an Alaskan husky walked up to us.

Hen eyed her with distaste.

"*Bonjour*," she said to us. "I spell my name with an *e* on the end."

We both gaped at her.

"Françoise," she said, opening her mouth wide.

"Oh," Hen said faintly. "Françoise," she repeated. "Of course." I saw her visibly square her shoulders. "*Bienvenu à Israël*," she said. I was impressed with her accent. "I hope your flight went smoothly."

"It was not good. Too crowded and the food was terrible."

"Hopefully things will go better for you now. I am Hen Canaan, this is my niece, Maya Laor." She gave me a nudge.

"*Bonjour*," I said. "*J'ai étudié français en école*."

"You speak French?"

It was on the tip of my tongue to tell her I just did. Instead, I did my best imitation of Hen's gracious, friendly smile.

"*Un peu,*" I said. "When I was ten, my best friend was French so I learned a little and I studied it in school. But it's been a long time since I spoke it."

"Perhaps you will get to practice now with me."

I smiled, showing very little of my teeth. "I hope so."

We led the way back to the car. I eyed her shoes. Black and rubber-soled, with severe square toes, as if the ends of her feet had been cut off. I was willing to forgive the poor choice of clothes—unflattering loose pants and a boxy shirt that hung to her thighs. Everyone liked to wear comfortable clothes on a plane. But there was no excuse for the shoes. I had a feeling this business trip wouldn't go well for Hen, in her stilettos and her sexy suit.

I smiled genuinely at Françoise. I had never seen Hen not get her way. I loved my aunt, but it was going to be a lot of fun seeing her handle this.

As we settled into Hen's sedan and starting driving to downtown Tel Aviv, a smell, faint at first but growing steadily stronger, began to fill the car. It smelled like a cross between moldy leather and crap.

Oh no, I thought. Someone stepped in dog poo. I tried to look discreetly at the bottoms of my shoes. Hen shot me a look of death in the rearview mirror, but I shook my head. It wasn't me.

After ten minutes, Hen was nearly gagging from the smell

and there was actually a faint red tint to the back of her neck. The air conditioning was on full blast.

I nearly laughed out loud. The more I fought to control it, the more it wanted to bubble out.

"I think we'd better pull over," Hen said, fighting for calm. "Fill up with some petrol, maybe get you something to drink. How does that sound?"

"*Oui*, that would be fine."

Once at the station, I saw Hen check her shoes. She glared at me.

"You can check them yourself," I said, showing her the bottoms of my shoes. "It's not me."

"It's coming from her," Hen hissed. "I could smell it in the car. Do you think she doesn't wipe her ass?"

"Are you sure it's not something in the car?"

"Yes," Hen said. "That stench is not coming from my car."

Françoise came shuffling toward us, holding a cola.

"Hold this, *s'il vous plaît*." She handed me her drink. Then she lifted her shirt, pulled out a money belt, and dropped the change inside. A powerful wave of that smell rolled over Hen and me like a tsunami.

"What in God's name is that?" Hen blurted out.

Françoise smiled proudly. "Pecorino," she said.

Hen blinked. "The cheese?"

"It's Italian. It is so very wonderful. I never travel anywhere without it."

Hen stood there for a moment, speechless, shaking her head like a horse plagued by flies. "What?"

"I put some pecorino in my money belt." She patted it like a pet. "Keeps my money safe. No thief will steal it with a smell like that."

"Oh my God."

Hen looked like she was going to cry.

"I read a lot before coming here. It is so very dangerous. I did not want anything to happen to me. A good friend told me about this little idea."

With Hen seeming to have lost the ability to speak, I felt I had to step in.

"A lot of what you hear in the news about Israel is exaggerated," I said. "We are a very modern country. You'll see, everything is online, our tech companies are at the forefront of the world. There is crime here, but that's like every place. We aren't going to take you anywhere dangerous. It's more dangerous to drive on the highway. Statistically there are more robberies in Paris than in Tel Aviv, more shootings in Washington, D.C., than in Jerusalem."

She sniffed at the mention of the States, as if to say, "What could you expect from that barbaric nation?"

"A woman can't be too careful. The bombings, the shootings," she waved a hand to encompass all sorts of bloodshed. "I wanted to take some steps to protect myself."

I wanted to ask her if pecorino had been known to stop shrapnel, but I didn't. I knew that people in other countries thought of us as a war-torn land, but it hurt to hear it firsthand. Israel had free speech, and journalists knew that Israel wouldn't throw them in jail, no matter what they said. But if they broadcast an anti-Arab segment, the Arab countries would never let them return. We got villainized, the bombers got victimized, and everyone else was too scared to visit. I wanted to shake Françoise until her greasy hair actually moved.

"But do not be concerned," she continued, completely oblivious. "I will not bring the pecorino to the meetings themselves."

Hen sagged with relief.

"Only when we are out on the streets."

We took Françoise to lunch at Shtut, my favorite outdoor café. It was only a block away from Hen's office. I was sure that if Hen had not sunk so deeply into black despair, she would have insisted on going to a fancier, five-star restaurant. But since I was (by default) in command, Shtut it was.

Shtut had bright-red strawberries painted throughout the café, on tables, chairs, the menu. Even the sun umbrellas were striped white and red. There were huge pots of flowering strawberry plants—the only plant, the menu explained, that could have leaves, flowers, and fruit at the same time. There was always some music playing, and the whole setup was so sweet and friendly that I loved coming here with friends. Even the name was charming, a play on words between silly, *shtoot,* and strawberry, *tut.* We all needed to relax just a bit. Sitting in the shade, a coolish breeze blowing, you couldn't picture anything wrong with the world.

I ordered a large salad with roasted peppers and eggplant. I assured Françoise this was very typical Israeli cuisine, and so she ordered it as well. Hen still hadn't said much since the gas station. I'd glance over at her from time to time, but she seemed to have sunk into a coma. She smiled and nodded, but claimed she'd forgotten all her English. I wondered if I should enter the diplomatic corps. It seemed I had an undiscovered talent for bullshit and biting my tongue.

Françoise and I chatted away as our waiter brought out our drinks. Ice water for me, white wine for Françoise and Hen. I hoped Hen wouldn't drink too much. She still had to drive. Unless she was so depressed she'd let me drive her gorgeous new Volvo? This would bear close watching.

A busboy came with a carafe of water. He set it on the table and looked at me for a moment.

"Thanks," I said, reaching for the water. He took it before I could reach it and poured the water for me.

He looked at me like I should know who he was, but I had never seen him before. He was young-looking, with a wispy little mustache, and he wore a white shirt and black pants like everyone else who worked at the restaurant. He set down the water and walked away without saying anything.

"He didn't pour any for me," Françoise said.

"Let me," I said, and poured for her.

After Hen had finished her first glass of wine and was nursing her second, she revived enough to remember some English, and I felt it was safe for me to slip away to the restroom.

On my way there, I saw the boy clearing a table. I felt his

eyes on me. I tried to figure out why he looked vaguely familiar. Was he an old schoolmate? A neighbor's cousin?

On my way back from the bathroom, I nearly collided with him. He almost dropped a tray full of dirty dishes.

"Careful," I said. "Steady." He steadied the tray, shot me a look, and sidled past me.

"Wait," I said. "Do I know you?"

"No, you don't know me."

Had I misunderstood his stare? I felt heat blooming up my face. Well, this was embarrassing. "Sorry, I thought you looked familiar."

"You think we all look alike, don't you?" he said. "Like dogs."

"What?" I would have taken a step back, except I was already up against the wall in the narrow corridor. "No. I saw you staring at me—" And then I knew who he was. He was the creepy guy from the bus. It was that look in his eye that reminded me, that same look of hate and disgust and fascination.

"Maybe I spit in your water," he said. "The way you Jews spit on me." It was dark in the narrow corridor. I felt claustrophobic. He couldn't be older than seventeen, didn't outweigh me by more than ten pounds. But my palms were clammy, my mouth dry.

"You didn't." I felt sick.

He smiled. "You're right. I didn't. Not in yours."

"Why?"

"Because you respected an Arab lady on the bus that night.

Most of you think we are the dirt that you wipe from your shoes at the end of the day. You live in the houses we build, you eat the food we grow, but you give us nothing for it. Where are the Palestinian shopping malls? Where are the Palestinian highways and hospitals?" He took a step toward me. "You have everything and we have nothing. You kill us every day. You think that can last? You think we will allow it? We will take what is ours. And then you will have nothing and we will just laugh when you beg us."

A waiter pushed past us to the kitchen and glared at the Palestinian.

"There are people out there waiting for their water," he said. "Stop wasting time. Get to work."

I felt like I was waking up from a nightmare, disoriented and scared.

The Palestinian glared at the waiter once his back was turned. Then he left without another word to me.

I walked back to our table, eyeing all the people in the courtyard who were drinking water, laughing, relaxing. When our food finally came, I toyed with it but didn't eat.

"This is wonderful," Françoise raved. "Lovely, just lovely."

I smiled, but I couldn't bring myself to taste it. The glistening oil on the roasted vegetables, the clumped mounds of feta cheese looked unappetizing and all I could picture was a long string of spit running from the boy's mouth to my plate.

When he finally came to clear our table, he smiled when he saw my full plate. I looked away and wouldn't look back until he left.

I tried to stay rational about this. Maybe he was just trying to gross me out. Maybe it was all talk. Then again, I saw that look in his eyes, that glitter of hate and malice. I completely shut out Hen's meaningless chatter, tried to ignore Françoise's stupid questions about how many taxicabs there were in Tel Aviv and how many restaurants served bread (because she had heard that Jews didn't eat bread).

I was trying to think. What should I do? The shitty smell of pecorino was still wafting through the air, and every once in a while I'd catch the scent. I caught Hen's eye and she just shrugged, game face on, in the zone, ready for anything. Finally lunch was over and, after Hen stepped on my foot under the table, I promised I'd meet them for dinner. As soon as they left, I went to find the manager.

I found him in a small back room and waited for him to get off the phone.

"I'm not sure that this is important, but I think you need to know that one of the busboys told me he spits in the water." My foot was tapping almost uncontrollably. I still hadn't fully decided if this was the right thing to do or a mistake.

The manager, a swarthy man in his thirties, wore a gold chain with CHAI on it, "life" in Hebrew. He turned and gave me his full attention.

"Who? What?"

I repeated myself. "I know it sounds strange, almost stupid. There's something not right about him." I hesitated. "He told me he hates Jews. He said something about taking everything back, making us pay." I met his eyes and I think we must have had identical looks of dismay on our faces. "This is serious, right?" I asked.

The day before, there had been a bombing in Petach Tikva.

"You're telling the truth." I wasn't sure if he was asking. I nodded.

"I'm a soldier. This is my favorite café. I would never make up something like this."

He rubbed a hand across his face, then raked both hands through his hair. He cursed.

"Okay, fine. I'll take care of it. You did the right thing, kid. You just can't be too careful, right?"

I described the busboy as well as I could. The manager wanted me to point him out.

"If it's the kid I think you mean, he's only been working here for a couple of months. I'm going to kill the guy who recommended him. But come, point him out."

I felt bad. I was getting this kid fired. He might be the only one earning a paycheck in his family, he might never get a job again. God, was this the right thing to do? And then, as we stood off in one corner, watching the restaurant, I saw him refill someone's water and I pointed to him.

"That's him. The one pouring water."

As if he felt my eyes on him, he turned and looked right at me. My finger was still extended, and my blood ran cold. His eyes narrowed. I dropped my arm.

The manager put a warm, heavy hand on the back of my neck. I jumped as if I had been shot.

"I have to leave," I said. "I've got to go."

"I'll take care of it," he said. "He won't be coming back here again."

I nodded and left, almost running, just wanting to get away from there. I spent the rest of the day feeling uneasy. I called Hen on her cell phone and told her I wasn't going to meet them for dinner. I went to work and just tried to forget the whole thing.

That night, I called Dov. I told him about Françoise and the pecorino and we both laughed.

"There's a meteor shower Friday. Want to go see it?" I asked.

"Sure," he said. I heard a smile in his voice and my toes curled. "But do you think it's safe, or should I bring some sardines to keep the thieves away?"

"Don't you dare," I laughed. "I've had enough stinky companions this week."

"All right, you win. The anchovies stay at home, but just this once."

That sick, guilty, uneasy feeling that had been with me all day slowly dissipated. I wished Dov was here with me, not just a voice on the line. I could almost touch that soft patch of skin by the corner of his eye, the rough stubble on his cheeks.

"I miss you," I said. "I can't wait to see you."

I decided not to tell him about the busboy. It was over. He was a freaky guy. I'd told the manager. The manager had surely fired him. That was it, end of story. There was no reason to rehash it. It wasn't something I was proud of.

"Good night, Maya," he said. I shivered because I loved the way his voice sounded when he said my name. "Sweet dreams."

"Sleep well," I said. "Dream of me."

That Friday, I laid out a blanket on the beach and we lay sprawled on our backs for an hour before the show began. I pointed out the constellations and told him their names. For the next two hours, debris left from the path of an ancient comet incinerated in fireworks. The tiny glowing particles streaked across the sky.

"Comets leave a trail of dust and grains of rock behind them as they fly by," I told him. "Like Hansel and Gretel in the woods. The comet leaves a path that marks its way in the sky. It follows the same path endlessly. Eternally. Circling around and around in its orbit for all time. And we just crossed through its path, and our atmosphere is burning up its markers."

He rolled from his back to his side and touched my face.

"So we're like the birds that ate the crumbs. Now the comet can't find its way home again?"

"Nah, this is just a tiny part of its orbit. It still knows the way."

"You're so smart."

I smiled but kept my eyes on the quiet sky, scanning it for more shooting stars.

"You remind me of a cat."

That got my attention. I looked at him. "Thanks a lot. How flattering."

"It's your eyes," he said. My sarcasm never did bother him. "They're a funny color. I've never seen anyone with eyes like that, except my mom's old cat."

I smacked him on the shoulder.

"Wait," he laughed. "Before you attack, hear me out."

"This had better be good."

"Her cat was pure black, not a spot of color anywhere, and very skinny." He rolled over and pinned me in the sand, meteors forgotten. "But her eyes were green and yellow." He lowered his head until our noses almost touched. "Like yours. They glowed in the dark." Supporting his weight on one elbow, hips still heavy on mine, he traced the outline of my eyes with one finger. I closed them and felt a butterfly-light caress on my eyelashes and around my eyes.

"I was creeping through the living room when I was a kid and I felt someone watching me. I turned around and saw two glowing eyes on top of the television. I nearly passed out."

I laughed.

He brushed hair out of my face and tucked it behind my ear. "But this cat was amazing. The most mysterious cat alive. She would disappear for days and then just show up again. We could never figure out where she went or how she got out in the first place. And then one day, when she had gotten old and slow and hardly went out anymore at all, she disappeared. We searched everywhere, put up posters, but we never saw her again." I kept my eyes closed and I could feel him watching me. "Sometimes I think I found her again when I'm with you." He eased himself down and cradled my face between his two hands. "And I keep thinking you're going to disappear."

Chapter Nine

VIRGINIA

"You want to know what it's like to live in Israel? It means checking out every person that comes on the bus. It means eyeing the bags lying on the floor at their feet, the shape of their jackets, the way their eyes scan the horizon."

It was late, and Payton and I both had had too much to drink. She sat on her bed and I sat on mine and I was thinking that if I were still in Israel, we'd both be sitting on the same bed. No one touched other people here, there was always a certain distance, even among friends.

"I got off a bus once because I was convinced one of the guys was a bomber." I was still in high school and I remember being almost frozen with fear, my racing heart. I was going to die. I had to get off. That moment of hesitation: Should I tell everyone else? But in the end, only I got off and the bus drove away and didn't explode. I walked twenty blocks in the shimmering June heat feeling foolish and shaky.

"You can't indulge your fears. You have to learn to ignore them, to be fatalistic. Or you'd never do anything. Never get out of bed, never go to work, never go out to see your friends, never leave your house." That was the power the bombers had. It wasn't just the body count that mattered. It was the fear that grew in everyone's heart that was so devastating.

That's actually what everyone said to me before I came here. They all said I just had to get on the bus again and trust, if not in God, then in the laws of statistics. Go to a café and enjoy a cup of coffee, a slice of cake, watching people hurry by. I would be fine. Don't let the bomber get you too.

But I couldn't do it. My aunt, my mother, and my dad basically dragged me out to dinner one night. I broke out in a cold sweat and refused to get out of the car. I saw danger everywhere. My instincts screamed that everyone looked suspicious. On some level, I knew I couldn't trust my instincts, but I wouldn't get out of the car. Hen kept urging me to move, just one foot out, then the other, and everything would be fine. My dad started yelling at her to stop pushing. She screamed at him to stop coddling me. My mom and I were both crying. Finally they gave up and we drove home again. It wasn't long after that night that I decided to leave Israel.

Payton sighed.

"It's so sad," she said. "I can't imagine living like that."

I shrugged. "You get used to anything. Besides, it's not like we have a choice."

Two empty bottles of cheap strawberry-flavored wine lay on their sides on the floor. Payton eyed them with distrust. We'd been drinking for about two hours and snacking on leftover candy from a party down the hall. I wasn't sure how I'd gotten started talking about Israel. It was the first time I'd really said anything about it to her. I had a pleasant buzzing in my head, and I fell silent, listening to it.

"I don't think that—" She stopped for a moment, as if listening to some inner voice. A wet-sounding belch suddenly erupted from deep inside her and I started laughing. Then I noticed that her face had turned colors. "I don't feel so good," she said, a hand pressed to her stomach.

"Are you going to be sick?"

"I don't think so." She took an unsteady breath. "But maybe."

The heaves started and I scrambled off my bed, grabbed her arm, and hustled her over to the bathroom.

"I'm fine," she said. "You don't need to do this." Then with a loud retch that echoed off the tiled bathroom wall, she dropped to her knees and vomited a massive amount of pinkish liquid mixed with half-digested chocolate and pretzels. I held her hair back off her face and neck. She retched until nothing came out but long, silvery lines of spit.

When most of the dry heaves had stopped, I wet a handful of paper towels and laid them on the back of her neck like my mother always did for me. Payton's face was red, and the violent retching had forced tears from her eyes.

"Leave me alone," she moaned, resting her head on the toilet seat. "I'm gonna die now."

"You're not dying," I said. "And I'm not leaving you."

I handed her a tissue, and she wiped her eyes and blew her nose.

"Let's get you up," I said, helping her stand. "Come on, let's go back to our room."

I flushed the toilet and then helped her over to the sink, where I made her wash her face and rinse out her mouth. We walked slowly back to the room and I got her into bed. She curled up on her side, hugging a pillow to her belly. I laid more cold towels on her temple and the back of her neck.

"That feels good," she said.

I turned off the lights.

"Thanks, Maya."

"Don't worry about it."

I made my way over to my bed and lay on it, not bothering to change out of my sweatpants into pajamas. It was quiet for a few moments, and I was sure that Payton had drifted off to sleep.

"Maya?"

"Yes, Payton. I'm here."

"I'm so glad we're roommates," she said, her voice blurred with alcohol and sleep.

"Me too." Then I was silent, barely able to make her out in the soft darkness, the fan in the window making its usual white-noise hum.

"Payton," I finally said, wondering if she was still awake.

"Mmm?"

"Why haven't you ever asked me about what happened in Israel?"

I thought I heard a soft laugh in the darkness.

"Didn't you know? In the South, we don't ask you why you've got a white elephant in your living room."

"What white elephant?"

"Exactly." I could hear the smile in her voice. "When you feel like telling me, you will. Until then, it's not my place to pry."

"Oh."

I heard the covers rustle as she shifted and snuggled deeper into her bed. "Good night, Maya."

"Good night."

My white elephant stood in the middle of the room, huge, silent, and impossible for me to ignore.

Chapter Ten

ISRAEL

I was heading into my last summer in the military and the heat started early and viciously. February and March had both been unusually hot and dry. By April, temperatures were soaring. Newspapers forecast a major drought. Politicians debated the costs of more desalinization plants to turn seawater to drinking water. Hot debates about the cost and benefits filled the papers, droned on television. Tempers flared quickly and malignantly, traffic snarls escalating into shouting and honking skirmishes.

I would collapse on my bed in the afternoon after work, drained from the hot bus ride home. The sun was intense, baking everything until the dirt cracked and flowers withered and died. I stopped wearing metal barrettes to hold my hair after I blistered my finger touching one. No matter how much I drank, I couldn't seem to stay hydrated, and the lines at the ice cream shop and juice stands were annoyingly long and pushy.

There was a sharp increase in traffic accidents, and the tempers of people without air-conditioning in their cars often snapped at the slightest provocation. Amid this bout of national goodwill, there was a spate of terrorist bombings. Most of them were in the territories and Jerusalem, but two were in Tel Aviv.

Everyone wanted to know what I planned to do after my service ended in June. I had applied for study in the United States months before and had just received an acceptance letter from the University of Virginia. I applied there after seeing the Rotunda in a friend's architecture textbook that cataloged one hundred of the most beautiful buildings in the world. After I'd gone online and seen that the school was well ranked and had an astronomy program, I decided, on a whim, to apply.

My aunt was purely against it.

"There are plenty of excellent universities here," Hen said. "And if you plan to live in Israel, you need to make your contacts here, not in the United States. It's all about who you know. That's how you get the good jobs. Don't waste this opportunity. It'll be much harder to succeed if you don't stay here."

My friends were making plans. Daphna wanted to travel through Thailand, maybe backpack in India, and have adventures that sounded great after tedious office work. Irit told me she and Leah were going to take a two-month trip through Europe. She invited me to come with them. But that wasn't what I wanted. I didn't want aimless travel, I didn't want to sleep in youth hostels or sell cheap jewelry on city streets. I wanted to really become a part of another culture, for my time there to have meaning.

Dov, of course, wanted to know where we stood. We both

knew that four years apart was too much. We wouldn't survive it. He couldn't come to Virginia with me, not if he wanted to make it in his uncle's company. If I wanted us to be together, I needed to stay with him in Israel.

"All your opportunities are here," he said. "If you want to go to school, you can. If you want to work, you can. But I can't work in Virginia. You're twenty years old. You need to decide what's important to you."

"I want to see the world. I want to get away from Israel, not from you . . ."

So we fought, and made up. And fought again.

"You're the one leaving," he would say when I cried. "Not me. All you have to do is stay."

But I couldn't. I had this burning desire to go, to study astronomy, to live in another language, to try something completely different. The days got hotter and hotter. Even at night, the roads and sidewalks pulsed with heat. Air conditioners broke, unable to keep up. Electricity prices rose, paralleling demand. It was too hot to think. I evaded my parents, who said I needed to make a decision and stick to it; evaded getting pinned down by my relatives and friends. At night, lying in bed, I tried not to move, to stay as still as possible as I felt drops of sweat bead on my skin.

My father, sensing that inertia would keep me in Israel, began to push for a decision one way or another. The deadline to let the university know my decision was approaching. By now there wasn't enough time to mail it; I would have to fax it to get it in on time. And still I didn't know what to do. The days were getting hotter, no rain, not even clouds to ease the piercing of the sun. Even the modest prayers for dew that are done in the summer (when even the Talmud teaches that it's useless to pray for rain) weren't having any effect.

I took to walking along the shore at night, something that gave both Hen and my parents palpitations—for once, they agreed. But I needed air. I needed space to think. I didn't know how you made a decision like this. Yes or no. Go or stay. So much riding on such small words.

In the end, I accepted my invitation to attend the University of Virginia.

After I decided, I slept one more night, a sort of eight-hour insurance policy to make sure I wasn't going to change my mind. I woke up and faxed in my acceptance from the office. I danced a little jig as it went through, feeling elated and nervous and weak-kneed.

I told Dov that we needed to talk. I didn't want to tell him over the phone. So we agreed to meet at Shtut. It had been almost a year since I'd gotten the busboy fired. At first I didn't want to go back. But after months had gone by, I missed it. I'd been back a dozen times by now.

I called home.

"I knew you'd go," my mom said when I told her.

"You couldn't have known that," I said. "I didn't know it."

"I knew," she said, "you wouldn't be able to resist the challenge. You never have since you were a baby and nearly crawled off the balcony."

"Are you okay with this?"

"Oh, *pashoshi*, you know I am."

"And you, *Abba?*"

"I couldn't be happier," he said from the other phone in the kitchen.

"You don't think it's too far away?"

"Telephones, Internet, plane tickets, Maya, the world is an awfully small place these days. You couldn't get too far away from us if you tried."

"I love you so much," I said. "You are amazing. Every time I think I finally understand you, that I know how you'll react, you surprise me."

My mother laughed. "Oh, honey, I hardly want to think what sort of narrow-minded people you think we are."

"It's our job," my father said, "to keep you on your toes."

I had a stupid grin on my face.

"Wow, oh wow. I can't believe I'm going." I was nearly hopping in place. Now that my parents knew, it was real. I could picture myself, a college student in America. My heart skipped a beat. "You wanted me to do this all along, didn't you?" I said. "You just didn't want to push me, right?"

"No," my father said. "We wanted you to choose what was right for you. You're an adult now. Whatever you chose would have been the right thing."

"I thought you might stay," my mom said. "Mostly because of Dov, but I'm glad you're going. I think this is one of those opportunities that you would regret passing up."

"Have you told him yet?" my dad asked.

That cooled my high. "No, I had to tell you first."

"I don't think he's going to be as happy."

"Yeah, I know," I said. "Okay, I'd better go. I said I'd meet him at four." I glanced at my watch. I had thirty minutes to get ready.

"So he gets to hear it face to face and we only get a phone call?" my mother said.

"*Ima*, don't."

"Just kidding, honey, just kidding."

I hung up, smiling. But I was worried about Dov. Would he really believe I was abandoning him by going to Virginia? I couldn't really blame him if he did. Maybe I would feel the same if I were the one staying behind. I loved him so much, and it hurt thinking we'd be apart for so long. But we could do it. If we really loved each other . . . I wondered if he would want to break up with me, and my breath hitched at the thought.

So. I washed my face and fixed my hair, leaving it mostly down, the way he liked it, even though it was hot. After a moment's hesitation, I went ahead and put on makeup. If I was going to find out he didn't really love me, if he was going to break up with me, then I wanted to look good. If he did love me, and if he did think we could do it, then I'd still look good. Besides, Hen was always urging me to put some on when I went out.

"You put clothes on your body," she said. "Why go out with your face naked?"

I still didn't exactly agree with her, but nearly two years of living with her had rubbed off on me.

No base, no powder, too damn hot for that, but I put on mascara and eyeliner, making my eyes slightly more catlike.

I decided to wear the rust colored halter top from the night of the party with the mayor. I slipped into a narrow black skirt and borrowed Hen's strappy black sandals, grateful once again that we wore the same shoe size. I didn't know what I would do when I moved out and wouldn't get to use all her great shoes.

I went into the kitchen for a glass of juice. What was the best way to tell him? God, this was so difficult. How could I make him see? And then before I could take a sip, the glass slipped through my fingers and I had time to say, "Damn it!" before it hit the ground.

There was a mess by my feet—broken glass, juice on the floor and the cabinets, dripping in red lines down my legs and on the sandals. Damn.

I mopped up the floor and wiped down the cabinets, making sure to get all the little slivers of glass because both Hen and I walked around barefoot. Then I went back to my room to figure out what to wear instead of the skirt and how to clean Hen's expensive sandals.

As soon as I stepped out of the apartment building, the heat hit me like a fist. My face prickled with beading sweat. The blacktop shimmered with heat, and I knew by the time I made it to Shtut, I'd be dripping.

Pearl, Hen's neighbor, was struggling with her bags of groceries. I glanced at my watch. It was already four. I ground my teeth and then hurried over to help her carry them in. She wanted to chat, but I was able to get away.

I hurried to the bus stop.

The bus arrived a few minutes later. I found a seat near the driver and hugged my purse. I tapped my foot impatiently and kept glancing at my watch. I hated being late. I really didn't want to keep him waiting. At the same time, I was elated. All this time I'd been scared to decide, afraid I would disappoint people who needed me. And yet my own parents supported me. I wanted to dance, I wanted to fly. This was finally the sort of adventure I'd dreamed about, doing something special and exciting. And it didn't have to hurt anyone. Like my father said, it was a small world these days. Maybe Dov and I could work it out. I could come back every summer. We would e-mail, call, visit. I wasn't a bad person, selfish and shallow. If this was really love, if this was meant to be, then it could work. If not, then what did it matter anyway? It was the first time I thought that I could actually have everything I wanted. Maybe I didn't have to choose.

We were stuck in traffic. I was now fifteen minutes late. We passed a small accident in the middle of the road. A man stood on the sidewalk crying, cradling his arm.

I was staring at him in surprise and in pity when I heard a loud boom. The windows on the bus rattled and I could feel the vibrations through the seat and all the way into my chest. There was shocked silence on the bus for a moment. Someone screamed.

"My God," I thought. "Something exploded."

Everyone on the bus started talking at once, trying to figure out what happened, where it happened. It was surreal. Someone said the mayor's office was nearby, the American embassy. Even though people were shouting and trying to see what happened, we all stayed on the bus. We didn't know what else to do. The traffic started moving again. Someone said maybe it was a car bomb. I could see over the driver's shoulder and suddenly I noticed a cloud of black smoke rising in the distance and it finally sank in that another terrorist had attacked.

This was the closest I had ever been to a bombing. I'd only seen their aftermath on television. I didn't know anyone else who'd ever seen one. I had actually heard the explosion. Goose bumps raced up my arms. I felt tears prickling. What was happening to my country? How could we live like this? How could this keep happening?

As the bus crept forward, we got closer and closer to the smoke. I could hear sirens behind us. The bus pulled up onto the curb to get out of the way. The driver turned on the radio, searching for news, but there was nothing about it yet, it was too soon.

Then my cell rang. I rummaged through my purse, pulled out the phone, and glanced at the readout. It was Hen.

"You won't believe what just happened," I said. I was upset and glad she called—I needed to tell someone about this.

"Maya, where are you?" Even through the fuzzy connection, I heard the edge of panic in her voice.

"On the bus, going to Shtut. Why?"

"Oh my God," she said. "Oh God, oh God."

"What?" I was totally floored. Hen was losing it. My skin broke out in chills. "Stop it! Stop saying that."

She wouldn't stop. She was sobbing.

"Hen, what happened!"

"Get off the bus!" she screamed in my ear. "Now! Maya, get off the damn bus!"

The bus was about to pull away from the curb.

"Okay." I was nearly crying now. I didn't know why. "Hen, I'm getting off, I'm getting off. It's okay. Don't cry. I'm getting off." The whole time she kept screaming "Get off now. Oh God, just get out of there!"

I stood up before the bus could lurch away, grabbed my purse, and with the phone pressed to my ear, I made my way to the door. "Can you hear me? Hen, listen! I'm getting off."

"Now, hurry, hurry, Maya." I had never heard her like this. My guts were coiling and my hands were clammy. I couldn't stop crying. I was feeding off her hysteria. I needed to breathe. I needed to calm down.

"Hen, please." I took an unsteady breath. "I'm okay. Where are you?"

The bus pulled away with a belch of black exhaust. The heat was still there, pressing on me. There was a bench, and I sat down.

"Are you off the bus?"

"Yes, Hen. I'm off the bus." I spoke slowly, but my chin trembled, I was so scared. There were sirens howling all around me. Ambulance and police racing to the scene, which I suddenly realized wasn't far from me. "What happened? Are you okay? Are my parents okay?"

My heart clenched at the thought that someone from my family could be hurt.

"Maya." She took a deep, unsteady breath. "There was a bombing at Shtut."

I felt nothing. Of all the things I was braced to hear, that wasn't one of them.

"What?"

"Don't you understand? There was a bombing. Now, five minutes ago. The guard at the office just told us." Her office was close to Shtut, I remembered.

"But I'm only four blocks away," I said. The numbness was fading. Still, it couldn't be. It didn't make sense. Shtut was off the main square. It was on a small street, a local café. Not the sort of target bombers go for.

"I knew you were going there today and I thought you said you'd be there at four." She started crying. "I—I ran over there b-but they wouldn't let me get near." She was sobbing. I could barely understand her.

"No," I said. "No. You're wrong. It couldn't be Shtut. It doesn't make sense."

"Excuse me?" I felt a cool hand on my shoulder. "Where was there a bombing?" I looked up. A middle-aged woman was looking at me.

"I don't know," I said, "maybe Café Shtut." But I still didn't believe it. "My boyfriend is there." As if that settled it. Nothing bad could happen if Dov was there.

And then I heard Hen say, "Oh, my love, I am so sorry. Shtut is destroyed. I saw it. It was Shtut."

I heard the pity in her voice and the anguish and I finally realized she was telling the truth. I'd been headed there. And if I hadn't been running late, I would have been there when the bomb went off.

"Hen, Dov was there. Waiting for me." I tried to swallow. "Did you see him?" My voice was rising as my throat tightened. "Did you see him when you went to look for me?" My voice was spiraling higher and higher. I felt that cool hand lift my damp hair, stroke my neck. The woman was still there, touching me, making hushing noises. I brushed away my tears.

"I don't know," Hen said. "I wasn't looking for him. No, I didn't see him. They wouldn't let anyone near. But you're safe, thank God. I thought you were dead. I thought you were dead, but they wouldn't let me look for you." She was crying again.

"Dov was meeting me there." My lips felt numb. I could barely talk. "Didn't you see him?" I couldn't stop asking. "How could you not see him?"

"No," she said again. "I couldn't get close. They didn't let anyone near."

The woman petting my hair looked at me with pity. I wanted to tell her that everything was okay. I knew what she thought.

"He's okay," I told her, dragging the back of my hand across my dripping nose, pressing the heel of my palm against my eyes. "Maybe he was running late too."

Other people had stopped, drawn by my crying, my rising voice, and the woman by my side.

"What happened?"

"Another bombing," she said. "This one thinks her boyfriend was there."

"God damn it," someone said. "Fucking terrorists."

I didn't want this. I didn't want them looking at me with pity, thinking I was a victim.

"Where was the hit?" one of them asked.

"Café Shtut," I said, fighting to be able to speak through the rising panic. "Café Shtut on Grossman."

There was a murmur around me.

"Your boyfriend was there?"

"I'm sure he's okay," I said. "I'm going to call him."

In fact, all around me, people were pulling out their cell phones, calling their kids, their friends, making sure no one had made the mistake of stopping by Shtut for an afternoon snack.

I hung up with Hen and dialed Dov's cell-phone number, but my fingers shook so badly it took me three tries. The call couldn't go through. I wanted to scream.

But it didn't mean anything. His phone could have been broken earlier today. He had dropped it before, had to buy a new one. Maybe the lines were down. Or maybe his phone was broken in the blast but he was fine. A million excuses ran through my mind.

He was fine, he was fine, he was fine. I wrapped my arms around my middle. I could hear people shouting on their cell phones, all able to get through, talking with their loved ones.

"He was there waiting for me," I said. The woman hugged me and pushed my head against her soft bosom and I sank in, hiding my face. I wrapped my arms around her and held on. I felt her arms gather me like a child.

"Shhh," she said. "Shhhh. There, there. It'll be okay. I promise. It'll be okay."

But it wasn't okay. Dov hadn't been late. He had been there, drinking a coffee, waiting for me to arrive.

Chapter Eleven

VIRGINIA

I stepped off the lit path and into the darkness of the shadows cast by the oak tree near the history-department building. The dark surrounded me, hiding me.

I studied the building in front of me, the lit doors and locked windows. It was fitting that the history department was in a distant, dusty building. History. Forgotten. I wondered if its location here was someone's idea of a joke. Chemistry, physics, even English and music were all at the heart of things, which is why I never stood in front of the School of Engineering thinking morose thoughts. I'm sure if I even tried, the building's cosmic aura of Newton's Laws of Thermodynamics would interfere, blocking transmission of such inconsequential nonsense.

Late at night, with the stars shining clearly above and the moon distant and cold, I was hidden beside the history department, haunted by my own history.

I stood for a moment under the tree, hands dug deep in the front pouch of my old hooded sweatshirt. With my dark hair and dark clothes, standing in the shadows I was perfectly camouflaged. As invisible as I could ever hope to be. I felt weightless. I could join the nighttime molecules, looking so much like them that I could be them. I felt safe in shadow, safer in disappearing than I ever could be in the light. With the darkness under my feet, no one could see me and I was free.

All the students I met seemed to fear the dark. They wanted to always stay in sunlight, on illuminated paths. The girls, especially, seemed to think that without streetlights they were at risk. Like children, I thought with disdain and envy. They didn't even realize that light could conceal far more than it ever revealed. It deceived you, tricked you, and lulled you straight into the heart of danger. Like moths, they gathered under streetlights to feel safe. My heart clenched when I passed them in the shadows, unseen and unheard amidst their giggles and shouts. They were so vulnerable. Anyone could harm them while they continued to think they were safe, surrounded by a force field of mere photons for defense.

The crisp night air was so different from the soft, featherlike feel of a Virginian summer night. I wondered what winter would feel like here. I had seen snow only once before, on a trip to France with my parents. My brother had raced to the elongated widows of our hotel room in Paris and said, "Look!"

The glass in the window was as old as the little hotel we were staying at, a warehouse from the eighteenth century. It was rippled, creating waves along its flat plane, distorting the view outside. It was what happened to glass over time.

For a moment, looking at the odd view from our window, I wasn't sure what I was seeing. I thought it was feathers floating down, that someone in the floors above us had a massive pillow fight. Or that all of the thousands of pigeons endemic to Paris had taken flight simultaneously, shedding the small downy feathers at their chests. Finally it clicked in my mind. My eyes made sense. Snow.

I looked forward to seeing snow again, though I was told it only fell here twice last winter.

Three students came stumbling out of a dorm room, reeling with drink, flushed with their youth and good fortune. It was Friday night, and lights from parties were cropping up like chicken-pox sores on the dark body of the university grounds.

I breathed the night air, tried to take pleasure in the clear night. The leaves had turned colors, though I couldn't see them in the dark. I couldn't get over how these ordinary-looking trees could produce such explosive changes. Trees never looked like that in Israel.

I didn't know why I returned to this thought so often—whether Israel had something or not. I guess I always felt that anything truly important or wonderful could be found in Israel. Maybe only in tiny quantities, but there nevertheless. When I thought about the beauty in Israel, the ocean, the pastel desert, I realized how much I missed it, and then I remembered that I was in exile.

A sudden shout of laughter made my heart race. Two guys guffawed and stumbled out of a West Range room, the historic graduate-student rooms off the Lawn. With the door open, I could see clearly into the small room, packed with people, full of music and light. I saw someone tilt a longneck beer bottle and swallow, come up for air, and laugh at a joke. I turned and veered off toward the gardens, walking slowly on the pale gravel path to reduce the noise of my footfalls. The undulating wall of tall, heavy trees created pockets of deep shadows and gloom.

I entered my favorite garden, seeking by memory the white bench at the curve of the brick fence. The moon was out, waxing half full. The trees threw shadows like dark veins on the smooth lawn. I found the bench, tucked romantically beneath the outspread limbs of a cedar tree, which was lush and green when everything else had started to wither and fade.

I closed my eyes, hoping to relax and listen to the small noises of the night, trying to recognize what was what.

Footsteps crunched on the gravel path outside the garden. I held my breath, listening. They stopped in front of the gate. Voices giggled, and the latch of the garden gate creaked open.

I scrambled off the bench and ducked behind it, my heart speeding as though I was doing something wrong. I peered over the bench at the intruders. How could someone else come into my garden? No one came here at night. No one but me. I didn't want to be seen. If I stood up and left, they would certainly ask questions.

They slipped in, clearly visible on the lawn, painted in silver, white, gray, and black, and looked around, making sure they were alone. Then they leaned into each other, slowly, and kissed. They were beautiful. They stood still, lips together, looking like ghosts. The moon outlined their forms, hid their faces. My heart slowed. One of his hands disappeared in her pale hair; the other clutched her close, then slid down her back.

I bit my lip, watching their kiss. It had never occurred to me before, but these secluded gardens were perfect for this sort of thing. My palms were sweaty and I wiped them on my jeans. Their kisses were growing intense. Her hands tugged at his belt.

I eyed the brick wall behind me, but it reached above my head. I could scale it but not silently. They would see me. They would be embarrassed, or scream, and I didn't want that. I was invisible. They would never know anyone saw what they did. I was night air. Settling down lower under cover, I peered through the painted slats of the bench.

I had forgotten what love looked like.

"Not out in the open, anyone could walk in and see us," whispered a breathless voice. "By the trees. In the shadows."

Don't, I wanted to tell her. Don't come any closer.

"I can't believe we're doing this." Her voice was excited. She tilted her head back, letting him kiss her neck. She laughed when he bent over her ear, kissing and nipping, large hands cupping her face like a mug of tea. I wished I had crept out. But now I was glued in place.

They dropped to the ground, too caught up in each other to bother with the bench after all. I looked away. I wouldn't watch. But my ears still heard, and I picked up the rustle of clothes coming off, the buzz of zippers opening. A shirt was thrown off, landing on the bench. I jumped.

A male voice whispered, but I couldn't hear what he said. I didn't want to. I didn't want to know their names. That, somehow, would make all this shameful. But without their names it was only exciting and rare, like two dancers who didn't know anyone was watching them. A soft laugh answered the whisper.

"You are so beautiful," he said.

I felt tears well up and I bit down hard, to stop a whimper from escaping. I hadn't made love in more than seven months. I hadn't touched an exposed belly, hadn't kissed that secret spot where someone's heart beats in the hollow of their throat, hadn't felt that free feeling of pressing up naked, chest to chest, arms twined around each other like a Celtic knot.

I suddenly had the urge to laugh, because this was too much. Because they were just kids and they were having fun, and what was I doing here, watching them, feeling my heart break again?

They lay still for a moment after they finished. They kissed and laughed and he helped her up. They both pulled up their pants and gathered the rest of their clothes. She picked up his shirt from the bench then turned away from me to give it back to him. She came so near to me I could have touched her.

He brushed the dirt and leaves off her back and kissed her again.

I waited for them to leave. They finally did, still giggling, whispering furiously, and giddy with daring. The sounds of their footsteps on the gravel path faded, tipsy laughter trailing after them like a banner. I crouched behind the bench, hunkered down in my makeshift bunker, feeling as though I had just fought a great battle. At last, the stillness I had come looking for returned to the garden. The smell of musty earth filled me and I let it calm me, steady and solid.

Finally I rose, stiff as an old woman, feeling the cold in my knees, in the long muscles of my thighs.

"*Aht cholah*," I said out loud. "You're sick."

What would it look like to someone floating above us, the young couple making love under a tree and me, crouched behind the bench, watching them like some goblin from a childhood tale? Watching and envying what I could not have. Tainting something lovely by my presence. I was ashamed. But I also felt lighter somehow, more at ease than when I'd first come in. They never saw me. I never disturbed them.

Were these excuses or facts?

I never realized how lovely two people could be, all that laughing between kisses, those tender caresses of love. Did I ever laugh when making love with Dov? I couldn't remember.

As I walked back, staying to the shadows, blending in, I felt like old glass, like viscous liquid was distorting my shape, rippling down my frame, pooling at the bottom. My vision was distorted, elongating, shrinking, depending on my density. I loved the night and at the same time I hated it. The night harbored secret and wonderful things to see and terrible truths to face if you were invisible like a ghost.

I slept in my bed for nearly a week after the night of the lovers in the garden, dreaming very peaceful dreams, feeling very refreshed and alert. I finished three assignments and even turned them in early. It was really amazing what I could accomplish if I actually slept. But by the sixth night, I was awake at midnight and staring at the ceiling, listening to Payton's breathing. I got up, dragged on my jeans and sweatshirt, and eased out of the darkened, sleep-heavy room.

Coming off a week of good sleeping, I would have thought that I wouldn't feel so tired now. As if I were a camel with humps that stored sleep instead of water. But in fact, my legs felt heavy and every step was an effort. I was angry at my body, or brain, or whatever it was causing this dysfunction. I was weary, but there was no sleep to be had.

I was too tired to walk up Observatory Hill, so I just kept walking anywhere the sidewalk was flat or sloped downward. My eyes burned, and my nose began to drip in the cool night air. In a few more weeks I'd need to buy a heavier jacket for walking at night. For once I wasn't alert as I walked. I didn't look at the stars, didn't hear the leaves rustling in the slight breeze. I just walked, doggedly, as if sleep were a destination I would arrive at. Eventually I found myself in front of the history department again.

I sat down under the oak tree, leaning against its craggy bark. I nearly fell asleep, but then the side door of the building opened, spilling light into the night, startling me.

I didn't recognize him immediately. With the light shining behind him, all I could make out was a dark silhouette, though it was obviously a man. He reached in and turned out the light in the hall, then locked the door behind him. He turned and I saw his face clearly illuminated by the security light above the door.

Justin.

I must have made a sound because he turned slightly and looked directly at me.

"Who's there?"

He couldn't see me. I was wearing dark clothes, in the shadows, and his eyes hadn't adjusted to the dark yet. I could have easily slipped away. Instead, I stood up and walked toward him.

"Hi, it's me," I said. I cleared my throat because my voice was rusty. "Working late?"

"Greenland." He raised an eyebrow at the sight of me. "What are you doing here?"

I shrugged. "Couldn't sleep, decided to stalk you." Not true, but maybe a part of me, a tiny little stupid part, hoped to see him. Maybe a part of me felt this meeting was inevitable.

He stepped closer to me but didn't rise to the bait.

"Are you okay? Is everything all right?"

"No," I said. "I'm fine."

He half lifted a hand, as if he wanted to touch me.

"You shouldn't be out here alone, it's not safe."

I snorted.

"Why are you hiding in the shadows?"

I shrugged again, trying for carelessness. I didn't want his pity.

"I wasn't hiding," I said. "I just can't sleep. Why are you still here?"

"My thesis is giving me fits. I thought I could work on it when the place was quiet, no distractions."

"Did it work?"

"No. The distractions seem to come from the research, not the secretaries." His features, in the orange light, were cast in copper and stone. It was hard to imagine him frustrated, unable to see his way. "Can I walk you home?"

I ignored the small fizz of pleasure at the offer.

"I'll be fine." He opened his mouth to protest. "I'm not ready to go back yet."

"Then let me stay with you. I'll worry about you, out here alone." He studied me in the meager light.

I turned my face away. I was annoyed and uncomfortable around him during the day, but now, in the dark, I didn't want to be alone.

"Fine, whatever," I finally said. "You can walk with me if you want to. It's no big deal."

I suddenly felt like walking. He walked beside me, his bag, heavy with notes, hung diagonally across his chest like a bike messenger's. We didn't talk much. Maybe he was thinking about his thesis. At one point he turned to me.

"You do this a lot, don't you?"

"Walk? Not sleep?"

"Yeah."

"I guess." I kicked a small rock and listened to it ricochet off the brick wall. We were nearing the garden where I'd seen the lovers. I didn't want to think about them, about what they would do here in my place.

"Did you always do it, or did something happen?"

At first I thought I wouldn't answer, but eventually I said, "Something happened a while ago." The grimness in my voice flustered me.

"Here, in Virginia?" A long pause. Then tentatively, "Or from before?"

"It happened in Israel, okay?"

I won't answer anything else, I thought. Not another question about this.

"Not Greenland?"

I laughed, surprised. "No, not in Greenland."

He didn't ask anything else.

We walked for a while, nearly an hour I guessed, though my watch had stopped working three days before. I kept wearing it to remind me to get it fixed.

I should ask him about his thesis, his research, I thought. But I didn't want to break the silence. Besides, I didn't really care. So I kept quiet and so did he, and we walked past the gardens and through one of the older residential neighborhoods near the university.

"I live here," he said, stopping in front of a brick duplex.

The mood between us that night was inexplicable. There was something quiet and calm. It was as if everything else in the world had disappeared in those early hours of the morning. No Dov, no Brook, no foreign customs, just him and me in the stillness before dawn.

"Do you want to come in?" he asked. He touched my hand. "You could try and sleep here if you wanted. I could take the couch."

I opened my mouth to say no.

Instead, I said, "I'm tired." And I was.

"Come in, Maya," he said. "Come inside and sleep."

I followed him, docile like a pet.

Inside, he leaned in and kissed me, like I knew he would. I kept expecting indignation to come, resistance at this man whom I hardly knew, taking away Dov's last kiss. But instead, I sank into the kiss and held him tightly. I was still thinking about the lovers in the garden. I was so tired of being alone, of aching for Dov.

The whole time, as we stumbled into his bedroom, as he undressed me, asking me if I was sure, I felt disembodied, floating above myself. Not judging. Just watching. Slightly curious about where all this would go, how it would be between us. I felt no embarrassment standing before him, studying his very nice body made of long lines of muscles and ridges, his stomach taut as an athlete's.

He held me afterward, a companionable arm around my shoulders. It was very late. The busy street that went through his neighborhood was silent. No cars, no students. Dawn would break soon, making this another night in which I hadn't slept. I shouldn't have come into his house.

"Listen," I finally said, after lying there silently. "Don't tell Brook."

"What a romantic thing to say."

"I'm serious."

"I know." He rolled over on his side, propped himself up on his elbow, and looked at me. "I shouldn't be surprised you'd say something like that, but I am. Are you ashamed?" His tone annoyed me.

"No." I sat up and kicked my legs to untangle the sheets. How could anyone irritate me this fast? "I'm not ashamed of anything I choose to do." A lie.

"Hey." He laughed and grabbed my arm to keep me in bed. "Easy."

"Let go." I struggled to get out of the bed. "I just want to keep this private. People would get the wrong idea." I glanced over at his smug face and wanted to get out of there. He tightened his grip on my arm, holding me in place.

"Let go, damn it!"

"Not until you calm down."

I blew my hair out of my face and looked at him straight in the eyes. If I had seen a glint of humor, I don't know what I would have done. But his face, inches away from mine, was serious, and the gray eyes fixed on mine were solemn. He was all but naked, lying next to me. I was finally embarrassed. What was I doing here? How did this happen?

"Justin," I said quietly. "Let me go."

He released my arms and sat up.

"Maya—"

"Stop." I held out a hand as if to prevent his words from reaching me. "Just stop. I don't want to talk." I pulled the sheet around me so that it covered my breasts. I rubbed a hand across my tired eyes. "I need to go. I need to sleep." I grabbed my sweatshirt from the floor. I didn't bother to look for my bra or my shirt. I just shoved my arms through and zipped it up.

"Maya, come on, we have to talk about this." The look of utter confusion on his face might have been funny if I wasn't so tired and sad. "What just happened here? What's wrong? You can't just leave like this."

"Watch me." I got out of bed, found my jeans, and yanked

them on. The denim was rough and slightly abrasive against my skin. I glanced over at him, avoided meeting his eyes. I made the mistake of looking at his bare chest.

I closed my eyes. I should never have slept with him. I didn't even like him.

"Come back to bed," he said softly. "Don't leave like this."

"That's not a good idea."

He got out of bed, slowly so as not to spook me. He touched my face lightly.

"I'm sorry," I said, turning my face away. "I can't do this."

"Don't be sorry," he murmured in my ear. "You haven't done anything wrong." I closed my eyes against his voice, his words. I wanted to believe those words. I wanted them to be true.

"You don't know," I said, my voice breaking on the words. "You don't know what I did." But I don't think he heard me.

He kissed my jaw, my eyelids, my lips.

"I'm sorry I upset you. Let me make it up to you." He pushed my hair off my face, tucking it carefully behind each ear. I was too tired for this. My sudden burst of energy and anger had left me drained.

"It's okay, Maya," he said so gently that I believed him. I rested my head against his chest and he put his arms around me and held me as if I could break.

Eventually the tears on the brink of falling receded. We went back to bed and I fell asleep spooned against him with his arms around me and his breath in my ear.

* * *

When I woke up later that morning, he wasn't in bed, which I was profoundly grateful for. I got up, intending to search for my clothes and get out of there. They were neatly folded on the chair in the corner. Jeans, panties, bra, shirt, sweatshirt, and my socks tucked in my boots under the chair. The image of him tiptoeing around the room while I slept, gathering my clothes, folding them, was unsettling.

I smelled coffee in the kitchen, and once I was fully dressed I peered in, but he wasn't there. The coffee pot was half full and there were a clean mug, a spoon, and a small jar of sugar placed on the counter, waiting for me. There was a dirty mug in the sink. I crept around the duplex, listening for him, but he wasn't there. Maybe he had more tact than I gave him credit for. Maybe he had a class to teach.

My stomach was a roiling mess and the last thing it could handle now was coffee. I debated about leaving him a note, but I couldn't figure out what to say, so I just left without writing one.

I hadn't slept very long in his apartment. From signs outside, it was not much past nine in the morning. The night before seemed surreal. Now that I was out on the street again, surrounded by people rushing here and there, laughing and arguing, I might as well have dreamed it all. Had I really slept with him? Had I made good on my stupid threat to steal him away from Brook? I blushed thinking about it.

I walked to West Main Street and called my room from the pay phone in front of the bank to see if Payton was there. But the phone just rang and rang until our answering machine picked up.

* * *

I looked for Justin the rest of the day but couldn't find him. I wondered briefly if he was avoiding me, but to give him credit, he didn't strike me as the type of person who would hide. He wasn't in his office, at the cafeteria, at home, or in the computer lab.

Around four in the afternoon, I ran into Brook while looking for Justin. When it rains, it pours, I thought sourly, noting her perfect golden hair, her caramel sweater and matching slacks. I, by comparison, was still wearing the jeans and sweatshirt from last night, had bags under my eyes large enough to carry my books in, and was so tired I felt like I'd been drugged. I had been debating whether I had the time to go to my dorm and nap when I saw her. My stomach sank. I expected her to walk by me without saying a word, but instead as she brushed past me, I heard her say, "Whore."

I stopped and stared at her, just like she wanted me to.

"Excuse me?"

She looked over her shoulder at me. "You're such a slut." Her perfect face reflected perfect scorn.

"He told you?" The shock must have shown on my face. A look of satisfaction bloomed across her face.

"You slept with him just to spite me. That's cheap."

Feeling like my face was frozen in horror, I walked away without saying anything. I wanted to kill him. I wanted to kill that bastard. It hadn't even been a full day since we'd slept together. He was a class-A bastard and I was off the hook. It was easy now; a part of me was even relieved. I didn't have to worry about falling in love or about hurting his feelings. He was a snake. That was what happened when you slept with snakes—they betrayed you.

I met Payton for dinner not long after that. My impulse from the morning to tell her about last night had faded. The less said about this gross mistake, the better; instead, I chatted about nothing in particular and made vague promises about weekend plans. I fought to stay patient as she told me about an irritating professor, fought to keep a steady face as she wandered off the topic and shared gossip about people I had never heard of. Finally I couldn't take it anymore. I cut Payton off in mid-sentence and made a lame excuse about a huge test coming up. From the look on her face, I didn't do a good job.

"I'm sorry, Payton, it's been a miserable day. We'll talk later, okay?"

She agreed, of course, because Payton always accepted an apology. But I saw that I had hurt her feelings, and she'd done nothing to deserve it. I left feeling even more depressed than before.

I walked to Alderman Library and spread out my books in a quiet corner on the fifth floor. I slid into the empty carrel and tried to concentrate on my astronomy text, studying solar wind. One day, spaceships might unfurl lightweight aluminized sails in space and literally sail through the galaxy on solar winds. I could see it so clearly, a three-masted ship made of glittering silver, gliding on currents of light. If I focused hard enough on that ethereal image, maybe I'd forget what a mess my life was.

I had been working for less than an hour when he found me. The first thing I noticed was a shadow over my notes. I looked up in alarm. I hadn't heard him come up.

"You scared me." I pressed a hand to my hammering heart.

Justin leaned against the carrel wall, arms folded over his chest, an amused little smile playing on his lips.

"How did you find me?"

"Your roommate Payton said you liked to study here." I choose to ignore the fact that he remembered Payton from that short meeting when we'd sat on the bench in the sun. I tried to ignore the weird luck that he'd run into her tonight, the fact he'd asked her where I was, and that he must have had to walk up and down the rows of books, going floor to floor, looking for me.

"Where have you been all day?" I asked. A trick question, of course.

"Been looking for me?" Again I saw that little smile, but this time there was a definite leer to it.

"Something like that."

"I went to Richmond to use the state archives. It's been planned for weeks."

"Oh."

"You didn't think I was avoiding you, did you?" The grin spread.

"No."

"No?" He raised a single eyebrow.

"No!"

"Good, because I wasn't. I've been thinking about you all day. We need to talk."

"That's right, we do. What the hell were you thinking?" Finally the frustration and humiliations of the day had found their target. I was almost shaking with a combination of emotions I couldn't begin to name. "Why did you tell Brook we slept together? I told you not to say anything to her. Was that too hard? You couldn't even wait a day?" I knew my voice was much too loud for the library. For all I knew, there were twenty students just on the other side of the bookcase—but I didn't care.

"First of all, you left something at my place." He reached into his pocket and drew out my watch. I looked down at my left wrist in surprise, but of course, it wasn't there.

"But how—" I never took my watch off.

"The watchband broke during the night." He managed not to smirk when he said that, but I felt my cheeks heat up. "I had it fixed and they put in a new battery since the old one was dead. Did you know you were walking around with a dead battery?"

"Yes," I said, momentarily sidetracked. "I didn't have the time to get it changed." He handed me the watch and I clutched it like a talisman.

"Second of all," he continued, "I didn't tell Brook we slept together, which is what you told me not to do. I just asked her if she'd seen you. She said no, but asked why I was looking. I told her about your watch. No harm done, the lady not compromised. You're a little paranoid, Maya."

Was it possible that Brook had just been guessing? Could it be that the look on my face just confirmed what she suspected but didn't know for sure? I gave myself a mental kick. It didn't matter.

"You knew very well what conclusions she would draw, and that's exactly what you wanted her to think." Nothing he said mattered. I couldn't let this continue.

"I can't help what she does or doesn't think," he said, finally showing some anger. "Look, Brook and I stopped dating months ago. Long before you ever came into the picture. We stayed friends, but that's all we are. Maybe we won't stay friends much longer if she can't deal with the fact I'm seeing someone else. But what she thinks shouldn't make a difference to you."

He was so deluded.

"All I'm saying—" I said.

"Maya, stop hiding. If you don't want to go out with me, that's fine. But you need to decide why, and it can't be because you think Brook has dibs.

"I like you a lot," he said. "I want to get to know you. I also think you're running away from something and, if you'd let me, I want to help. I want to know what happened. If you still think sleeping with me was a mistake, if you don't want to go out with me, I think I deserve a better reason than because of Brook."

"You have a very high opinion of yourself," I said, heading for the jugular. "Maybe I just don't like you. Maybe I was just looking for a one-night stand."

"Maybe," he agreed. "But why choose someone you know, someone you're going to have to see every week until the semester ends? For a bright girl, that was a stupid thing to do."

"You don't know what you're talking about."

"Don't I?"

I took a deep breath.

"Why are you doing this?" I asked. "I made a mistake last night. I just want to forget it ever happened. Why won't you let me?"

"Because I see you're hurting and it started long before me." He stopped himself. "I want to know what happened to you. And last night—" he shook his head. "Maybe you're right. Maybe it was a mistake. I don't think so. But you clearly do. And I'm sorry for that."

I looked away from him, from his classic good looks, his wrinkle-free khakis, his well-meaning eyes and easy life. My heart ached and I curled my fingers inward, digging my nails into my palms to steady myself. Exactly the same move I made at Dov's funeral to keep me standing straight as I felt every glance, every tear, shred me further.

"My past is none of your business," I said as coldly as I could. "And morbid curiosity is not a reason to start a relationship. Flattering as that is."

He looked at me in silence. I met his gaze. Held it. I saw his face close, his eyes shut down, and I knew I had won.

"That's how you want it? A cheap one-night stand? Fine." He straightened from his slouch against the wall, shoved his hands into his pockets. "Sorry it took me a while, but now I get it."

He walked away, and I stared at his retreating back, listening to his quiet footsteps until he reached the staircase, and then I heard only the hum of the vents above my carrel.

I uncurled my hands and watched the blood fill in the little half-moon indents. I noticed that he'd chosen the same chestnut color for my new watchband. I wanted to cry.

"Fuck," I said, relishing the word. It was one of those English words that just rolled off my tongue.

Then I took some deep breaths à la Daphna and her yogis. There was a reason for this. I could not be in a relationship again. Safer, better to be alone. I'd transfer out of his discussion section in the morning. I couldn't imagine facing him in class, giving my opinion on the importance of the Marshall Plan.

I put Justin firmly out of my mind and spent the next three hours reading how one day the sun will become a red giant and grow so large it will engulf Mercury. Sometimes there was nothing better than astronomy to put things in perspective.

Chapter Twelve

ISRAEL

Once when I was very young, I woke up in the middle of the night. I was lying perfectly still in my narrow bed, afraid to move but not sure why. Then I saw it. Two burning red eyes glared at me from above my dresser. When my eyes adjusted to the nighttime gloom, I saw the rest of it. It was the size of a large cat, with four paws that had wickedly curved claws, huge black nostrils that flared at the scent of me, and those red eyes shaped like lemon wedges glowing in the dark. I must have made a sound, because its massive head turned toward me and it raised its black lips in a soundless snarl. Its jagged teeth were like a mouthful of nails. I screamed and, finally able to move, I hurled myself out of bed and tore off to my parents' bedroom, expecting at any moment to be attacked from behind. I made it to their room, launched myself between their two sleeping lumps, and burrowed under their warm covers.

Of course, when they heard my story, they soothed me and said that it was just a dream. No such thing as monsters, they promised; it was just my imagination. But I knew the difference. I refused to return to my bed and spent the rest of the night with them.

Afterward, when I returned in daylight to my room, I carefully approached my dresser. There was no sign of the monster at first. It had left no scratches or claw marks or coarse black hairs sharp at the ends like needles. But I looked closer, my face so close to the dresser that I could see the whorls of the grain in the wood. When I was only millimeters away from where it had crouched in the middle of the night, watching me sleep, I noticed a smell. In itself it was not unpleasant, a mix of cloves and allspice, but underneath there was something sickly sweet. Like the peach that had rolled behind our stove and lay there, forgotten for a week, until it blossomed with rot.

I drew back in alarm. There was my proof. I dragged my parents in, demanded that they sniff, that they smell it and know it was real. But they smelled nothing. No one could smell it but me.

That is what it was like when Dov was killed. No one believed me. No one would listen when I said it was my fault. Another nightmare. Another monster. They kept insisting it wasn't real.

It was so hot and bright during Dov's funeral that sweat dripped down everyone's faces like tears. Sweat stains bloomed on the backs of people's shirts and under their arms. I kept my sunglasses on because I couldn't bear to look at anything without a dark shield. I was a murderer. I was attending my victim's funeral, and people were consoling me. I wasn't sure how much worse it could get.

There were three other funerals at the same time. All victims of the same bombing. There were not many cemeteries to choose from, even in Tel Aviv. I watched the other groups because it was easier. Each open grave had nearly a hundred people huddled around it. I wondered why the other victims had chosen Café Shtut that afternoon. Were they meeting someone there too? Would everyone here still be alive if I had never spoken with the manager, if I had never gotten that boy fired?

It was so hot that I felt sick. I fought back a wave of nausea and my skin prickled with heat and goose bumps. The hair on my arms was standing up. My father put his arm around me and I could feel his sweat seep through my shirt to my shoulder. My mother held my hand. Dov's mother buried her head in her husband's chest. He was not in the office today. I could see his whole body convulsing with sobs.

The rabbi cut Dov's parents' shirts as a sign of their mourning. And it was over. We stumbled out of the cemetery. His parents would start sitting shivah at their home. I would go see them later. But not yet. Not now, when they still had dirt from their son's grave on their shoes.

"It's not your fault," Hen said. It was two months after Dov's funeral. I had just come back from a run. It was June, and the heat was brutal. My legs were shaking and my shirt actually dripped with sweat. The air-conditioned apartment was freezing after the heat outside, and I was shivering, trying to keep my teeth from chattering. "Stop hurting yourself. Stop punishing yourself." She grabbed my arm, and her nails dug painfully into my skin.

I hadn't decided if I should go to the States. My father had already paid for the first semester, but every day, every hour, I changed my mind. Sometimes it seemed like the right sort of punishment. After all, Dov had been there waiting to hear what I had decided. Dov had wanted me to stay. I should stay. But then sometimes I thought if I stayed here one more day I would die too.

There had been another suicide bombing the day before. Dozens of people had been injured. Two killed. Not a bad one, considering.

"I know what you're doing," she said, giving me a little shake. "You do this every time there's another bombing."

"What are you talking about?" I jerked my arm out of her grip. I walked to the kitchen and filled a glass with water.

"Every time there's a bombing you hurt yourself. You torture yourself, soaking up all the details on television, reading all the articles. Then you punish yourself. You don't eat. You run in this crazy heat. You don't sleep. Why do you do this to yourself?"

"I just went for a run." I said. "I don't know what the hell you're talking about." My teeth were chattering now. I clutched my arms to my chest to preserve body warmth, but my shirt was clammy and it didn't help.

"Stop being a victim. Get over it!" Hen's patience with me had finally snapped. "Everyone loses people they love. Stop wishing you'd been there. You weren't. And you know something, I'm glad you weren't. That's right." She jabbed a finger in my chest. "To me, that's a blessed miracle. Yes. Dov was there. Sad. Tragic. But that's life."

"No, that's life in Israel!"

"Then go. Leave. Stop hiding behind Dov's death, don't make excuses. If you want to go, then go. But if you stay, you have to start living life in this world again. I hear you on the phone, always refusing to make plans, to meet your friends. You have to start living like a human being and not like a dog in a cage. You think no one noticed?"

I hated her. Hated her shallow views, her simple life.

"I am not living with you anymore," I said.

I got up, grabbed my purse, and slammed the door on my way out. I called Daphna—my only friend who owned a car—on my cell phone and she drove me all the way back to Haifa, back to my parents. They drove up the next day and picked up the rest of my things from Hen's. I don't know what they said to her. I didn't ask and they didn't say.

"It's not your fault," my parents kept saying. They had more patience for me. They said it every day, every morning when I stumbled into the kitchen for my morning coffee. I had been excused from the rest of my military duty. I only had a few weeks left anyway. So I lived at home and did nothing. Didn't get a job. Didn't meet friends. Didn't sleep. When my welcome packet from the University of Virginia arrived, I was surprised. Surprised they still expected me. But I had faxed in my acceptance an hour before Dov was killed. The welcome packet sat on my desk, unopened.

"You have to start sleeping," my mother said. I could hear the tears in her voice. "Maya, my love, stop hurting yourself. It wasn't your fault."

They made me see a shrink.

"Not your fault," the counselor said. She specialized in terror survivors. She had plenty of experience with this sort of behavior. I was surprised she even had time to squeeze me into her busy schedule. Too many survivors. "It's typical for victims to try to take on the guilt of the perpetrator." She spoke in a very matter-of-fact tone. No coddling here. "But don't you do it. You're not the one who detonated a bomb in the middle of a crowded café. You are not the terrorist. You are a person trying to live her life the best she can. Yes, a terrible tragedy happened. Don't make it worse. Seven people already lost their lives to this bomber. Don't let yours be the eighth."

I sat in her sunny office and let her talk. I knew she believed what she said. Intellectually I could understand what she said. I agreed with her. It was true for most people. But it didn't matter in my case. I didn't even bother to explain. It was different. After he was fired from Shtut, he never got another job. He just sat at home, fuming and plotting. He was eighteen. Unemployed. Full of rage. Because of me. If I hadn't said anything, maybe he would still be working, still bringing money home to his parents, hating the Jews, but beholden to us for his living. Once that was taken away, he didn't need us anymore.

I created many scenarios where the ending was different. There were so many ways this could have been averted. If Dov and I had agreed to meet later. If I called to say I was running late and for Dov to come meet me. If I let Dov choose the place where we met. If that goddamn manager had handled the situation differently. If I never said anything to the manager. If that stupid Frenchwoman hadn't brought pecorino in her bag, Hen would never have agreed to go to Shtut for lunch. If. If. If.

It didn't matter what anyone said. If Dov and I had never met, he'd be alive today. He wouldn't have been at the café and he'd be alive. But he did go and I had told him to meet me there, and now he was dead. Those were black-and-white facts. Meeting me, falling in love with me, was the worst thing that ever happened to him. That didn't even take into account that I was meeting him to tell him I was leaving for four years.

My parents, my aunt, the counselor could repeat their mantra as much as they like, but I knew the truth.

Besides, I wasn't sure Dov's parents didn't agree with me.

I saw them a few times after the funeral. I wondered if they hated me.

My parents drove me to the airport at the end of August. We were quiet in the car, mostly. There was not much left to say. I was going to the United States because none of us could think of anything else I could do. It was almost four months since Dov had died. My parents hoped sending me away was the right thing to do. But I knew they were scared that once I got away from them, I might do something stupid. Something harmful. I knew I wouldn't, but nothing I said could make them believe that. I could sense their doubts, their fears, like a smell in the car. They were fighting a battle for me, trying to at least, but there wasn't anything they could do and we all knew it. Keeping me near wasn't working, and they were taking a chance that sending me away would help.

I said good-bye to Adam at home. I knew he was confused about the whole thing. Mad and sad about Dov, but not really understanding me. That was okay, though. I didn't really understand me either.

"You take care, little brother," I said. He was taller than I was now. He'd grown a lot in the past two years.

"You too, big sister."

When he kissed me on the cheek, I noticed that his skin was rough with patches of stubble. I hadn't even noticed that he'd started shaving. He noticed my look and rubbed his chin with sheepish pride.

"Guess it's time for my weekly shave."

"Adam," I laughed. "I love you so much. I'm going to miss you."

"I know," he said, and his mouth twisted with something I couldn't read. "But I'll miss you more."

We drove under blue skies with only a few white clouds to mar perfection. My mother sighed a bit and my father kept glancing at her.

"I'll be fine, *Ima*," I said.

"I know."

"Do you?"

"If it doesn't work out," my father said, "just come back to us. Don't force yourself through this if it isn't right for you."

He had his doubts that I should leave my support when I needed it most. But even he could see staying here wasn't good. My mother had convinced him I should go. Maybe she was right. Maybe leaving would be better. I didn't think it could get worse.

"I'll be fine, *Abba*."

"I know you will. I just want you to know."

"I know," I said. That didn't seem like enough. "Thank you."

"I miss you already," my mother said in a small voice.

"Oh, *Ima*," I said. "I miss you too."

"All this missing and she hasn't even boarded a plane yet," my father said.

We laughed weakly.

"It's for the best," my mother said. "You need a break. You need some peace."

I sat in the backseat watching the fields and orchards and towns on the side of the road whoosh by, appearing and disappearing, rolling away with ease.

There had been another bombing that morning. They didn't want me to know about it, but I heard the news during breakfast. It was in Jerusalem. They kept thinking I was going to fall apart every time there was another attack. Everyone thought so. They tried to keep it from me. My mother even canceled our newspaper subscription. They never turned on the television when I was around.

"It won't always feel like this," my mother said. "And going to the States, it's so exciting. You'll have such a good education, make new friends."

"Getting away from Israel is the only reason I'm doing this," I said. I hated myself for saying mean things. It just hurt them more. But the words seemed to spill out. "You know it and I know it. It has nothing to do with friends or adventures or even learning anything. I just have to get out of here."

We didn't say much after that. There were so many things I wanted to say. Bitter words. But it wasn't their fault. It wasn't fair for me to hurt them more. I managed to keep silent and they kept quiet too. My parents insisted on coming in the terminal with me, and they stood beside me until I went through passport control, where only ticketed passengers could go. My father nearly crushed me in his hug, and I felt my mother's soft lips on my face, near my eye. Once I was past the metal detectors, I turned back and waved at them.

"*Shalom*," my mother called out. A few people looked at her. It was an old-fashioned way to say good-bye. It meant hello and peace as well.

"Be safe," my father said.

"I love you," my mother said.

I waved one last time and walked away.

I left them standing so close to each other they were nearly touching.

I left Israel, flying away in a 747, leaving only a fading contrail to mark my passing. I told myself, in a litany on the plane, that it was for the best.

The plane trip was uneventful. A large, dark group of Hasidic men took up the back half of the El-Al flight. They would get up at certain mysterious intervals and pray in the back of the plane, near the bathrooms. I wondered how they knew which time zone to pray by—the one they came from, the one they were headed toward, the one they were currently flying through, or some combination of all three. I was sure they had debated this for many hours back in Israel and that they reached a logical, Torah-based conclusion. I was vaguely curious about what they decided and the rationale behind it, but not enough to ask any of them. I always felt uneasy around the Hasidic community, the men with their thick beards and thicker black coats, the women with their styled wigs and long skirts.

On this trip, however, I enjoyed the sound of their deep, prayerful murmurs from the back of the plane, rising above the hum of the engines. I leaned my forehead against the cold plastic window and gazed out at nothing.

I tried not to think of my last night in Haifa as a bad omen. I had cramps and the room was too hot. I was covered in a sticky sheen of sweat. It took me a moment before I realized what the wetness between my legs was. My period had started early. I turned on the light by my bed and saw dark blood, almost black, smeared on the sheets and my shorts. It was three in the morning. I stripped the bed, stripped off my shorts, and after cleaning myself, I spent nearly half an hour scrubbing out the blood from my pajamas and my mother's sheets.

The murmurs of prayers from the back of the plane had faded, and there was only the hum of the engines for company.

The sun had set, and my reflection in the window stared back at me. I was headed someplace new and different. I was going there alone. I prayed then, something I rarely did. I prayed on the plane for God to help me and keep me and make me whole again.

Chapter Thirteen

VIRGINIA

By January, the start of my second semester, my body was wasting into air, becoming air. I began to ache at night. I dreamed of kissing Dov, of brushing my lips over his, of him kissing my forehead, my nose, my face, my neck, my shoulders. I dreamed of tracing that delicate pale path from tan wrist to ivory shoulder. I could feel his mouth on mine, his warmth, and I let my fingers glide along the hills and valleys of his stomach and his back, felt his weight on top of me, inside me. I would cry out in my dream, so happy he was back, that it had all been a nightmare, his death, my guilt. He was back with me, touching me, loving me, and everything was all right. I would wake up crying, alone, tangled in my bedsheets.

On mornings after nights like that, I functioned a little slower and my temper came a little faster. I was raw and unable to deal with the eccentricities of the people around me.

My parents and Adam had come during winter break, and we'd spent two weeks together. We spent the first few days in Charlottesville, so they could see the university and where I lived, and then a week and a half in Florida, where everything was sunny and bright and warm.

When I was with them in Miami, it seemed like everything

was going to be fine. It felt like we were back in Israel, hanging out by the water on a Friday afternoon. We ate ice cream every day, went to see an alligator farm, spent a day at Disney World and got our picture taken with Goofy. I laughed at Adam's jokes, and my parents lost that tight look around their eyes. At the airport, we said good-bye. They were flying to Israel. I was flying back to Virginia.

"Well," my mother said, stroking my hair. "I guess things are working out fine."

"Yes, they are," I said, and I meant it. At least for that moment, everything seemed fine.

But after they left, I was back, living in the gloom. The days were short and gray. The nights were long and cold. I began to really regret coming to Virginia. I missed them so much and I ached to be warm, to be home again and not so far away.

I hadn't spoken with Justin since our fight in the library. I had switched out of his section—a bureaucratic mess—and I didn't have a class with him this semester. I didn't walk by the history department at night anymore. If I could run away from my homeland, it was a simple matter to retreat from one human being.

One night, Tiffany, my hallmate and sometime friend, was getting ready for yet another party. She stopped by my room and invited me to come.

"It's a frat mixer and I think you'll really like it. There're some really cool guys there and you've never really met my sisters. A bunch of them will be there." Tiffany had rushed at the same time that Payton had and been inducted into a sorority, though not the same one. Payton was gone for the weekend, on some sort of retreat, and I had the room to myself. But for once, I wasn't looking forward to solitude.

"I don't know," I told her, rubbing my face. "I'm pretty busy."

"Oh, just come. If you've never been to a frat party before, you have to give it a chance. It's part of the college experience."

I had been feeling low that day, and the thought of spending the evening alone with my stars and galaxies wasn't a cheering one. I missed Dov at the oddest times. Not exactly grieving for him, just missing him. I missed my boyfriend, who was funny and smart and knew me so well.

"All right," I said. "I'll come." She cheered and I smiled. "What do I need to wear?"

I went to my first fraternity party in tight black pants and a skimpy, shimmering shirt, walking quickly and shivering in the cold January night. On Tiffany's advice I didn't bring a coat, because it'd be hot inside the party and there'd be no place to leave it. When we got there, the party was well under way. The house almost shook under the blast of music, and the smell of spilled beer greeted us before we got to the door. I followed Tiffany as she pushed and maneuvered past the press of bodies at the door.

"First things first," she yelled at me through the music. Her streaked brown hair looked gray in the flashing lights. "Beer."

I nodded and followed as she made her way to the beer

line. I stood there, slightly swaying to the earsplitting music, waiting for her to come back. A few minutes later, she was there with my beer. We clinked the red plastic cups together.

"Cheers," she yelled.

"Cheers." I forced myself to match her grin.

I swallowed the beer in quick gulps for courage, for oblivion, and because it didn't taste very good. It helped me feel reckless. I wanted to forget everything.

Tiffany started dancing to the beat, swaying and undulating her arms above her head.

"Where can I get another beer?" I yelled in her ear.

She whooped a cry of encouragement and pointed to a crowded corner in the rear. I didn't get very far before a guy wearing a tattered baseball cap asked me if I needed more beer. I nodded and off he went, gamely pushing his way through the crowd. He made his way back to me, a triumphant beer held up like the Olympic torch. Tiffany had moved over and was huddled with a group of her sorority sisters, eyeing a nearby group of guys.

"Thanks," I told him. I figured he'd be off to find another thirsty damsel in distress, but he stayed with me and we sort of danced, each holding a large plastic cup of lukewarm beer, not really bothering to talk above the ear-blasting music. He was taller than I was, narrow and thin. In the dim light I could not tell the color of his hair or eyes.

I finished the beer in my hand and he offered to get me another one.

"I'm fine," I yelled. "Thanks."

"Aw, come on," he shouted. "How about I bring you one, but you don't have to drink it if you don't want to?"

I smiled at him, and off he went into the crowd for more beer. He was so friendly and he stood so close. When he leaned to talk into my ear, he touched my face lightly. It felt good to be close and to touch him effortlessly on the arm as I leaned in to hear what he was saying. I ended up drinking the beer he brought me and the one after that. The music was loud and the deafening bass of the anonymous song the speakers were blaring vibrated pleasantly in my stomach. It was dim in the frat house. As the night wore on, faces blended into one another. At one point, Tiffany tapped my shoulder.

"We're going to Saint Elmo's," she yelled in my ear. "Are you coming?"

"No," I yelled. "I'm staying."

"See you later, girlie!" She winked at me, gave a thumbs-up to the guy I was dancing with, and left.

We kept dancing, a little closer now. He smelled good, like soap. I closed my eyes and leaned into his shoulder.

When I told him I was too hot to dance anymore, he suggested we go upstairs.

"I'm a brother here," he said with some pride. "I have a room upstairs."

I can't say that I didn't know what he meant or what it would lead to. It wasn't that I'd had too much to drink or that I didn't know what I was doing. I did. I wanted to. I thought, a little viciously, that this is what Justin meant, right? A one-night stand with a stranger. I'd never done it before. Might as well give that a try, since nothing else seemed to work. So I jogged up the steps, following him.

It was a little cleaner upstairs; the floor wasn't slick and sticky with spilled beer, but it was grimy with dirt and dust. I could feel tiny pieces of what seemed like sand, but couldn't have been, grind under the thin soles of my shoes. He unlocked his room, but he didn't turn on the lights.

I thought I could make out a desk, a pile of clothes on a chair, and a bed only slightly rumpled. We sat down on the bed. He took off his hat and ran his fingers through his hair.

"You're really pretty," he tried. "Um, your eyes are so amazing."

"Don't," I said, touching his arm. "Don't talk."

He leaned over and kissed me tentatively on the lips. After a moment, his tongue edged inside. I kissed him back. I could feel his heart racing. The sounds from the party below were coming in muted but clear. The room was very dark, with stripes of light from a street lamp seeping in through the blinds. We lay down on his bed. I closed my eyes.

I woke up at five in the morning, not tangled in sheets but lying side by side with a boy whose name I didn't know. I eased off his narrow bed as quietly as I could, taking care not to touch him as I slipped out from under the covers. I had a headache from the beer and my mouth felt coated in fuzzy lint.

I felt stupid and disgusting. This was the first time in my life that I hadn't made love with a guy, just had sex. I'd never realized the difference before. With Justin, it had been different. It had been tender and loving. But this . . . I looked over at the boy. His face was turned toward the wall. This was a mistake.

I gathered my clothes and put them on. He rolled over and I glanced at him to make sure he was still asleep. I wasn't sure I'd ever told him my name. I don't think he ever asked.

The stairs creaked with every step, sending trills of alarm through me. I eased open the front door, left unlocked for guests like me. My steps echoed softly down the dark street, the sunrise still hours away. I had never felt so alone. The trees loomed over Colonial-style mansions, each home to a different sorority or fraternity. I hunched my shoulders, trying to keep warm. Several meters ahead of me was another figure, slowly walking home. The walk of shame, I had heard someone call this. I had laughed at it then. I did not find it funny now.

Tiffany grinned at me later that day when I ran into her in the stairway. Grinned at me like we'd just shared a wicked little adventure.

"So I'm guessing you enjoyed your first frat party?"

I managed to stifle a snarl. Barely.

I don't remember what I answered. I returned to my books and tried to take comfort in my stars. They provided no warmth, but no shame either. I tried to find delight in the rings of Saturn, the moons of Jupiter. My nights were even more restless than before. I couldn't close my eyes without summoning up the picture I must have made, sleeping with the boy who smelled like soap and beer. My face would flush and I would roll over, burying my head in the cool pillow, as if to block out the sight.

Payton returned Sunday night, full of stories about her weekend. I let her talk. I felt like shit. Her stories about a ropes course and a food fight seemed like they belonged in an alternate universe. How could such things exist?

"How was your weekend?" she asked.

"You know," I shrugged. "Like always."

"You've got to get out more," she said. "There are so many amazing things going on every weekend, you've got to get involved."

"Sure. You're right."

"Maybe you should join a sorority," she said, eyes wide. "Wouldn't that be fun?"

I gave her a look.

"You might like it, you know."

But she didn't pursue it and neither did I. She finally fell asleep, and I stayed huddled on my bed, feeling old and guilty, a dark blot of a person amidst sunny yellow swirls.

The next day, my father called and told me that Adam had applied to join a combat unit the next year. The bottom of my heart fell out. I barely managed to stay in my chair.

"He can't," I said. "You can't let him."

"I can't stop him."

"You have to. He'll be killed! How can you let that happen?" I was trying to be cruel. "Don't you think enough people have been hurt?"

I didn't know what I would do if my little brother was killed as well. Could God work like that? Would Adam pay for my sins? Or maybe, the thought occurred to me, he felt he needed to avenge Dov's death?

"He's grown up. He isn't a child and he knows what he wants."

"This is because of Dov," I said, my voice shaking. "This is because he wants revenge. Tell him not to be an idiot. Tell him—"

"Stop it, Maya." There was steel in my father's voice.

I stopped.

"Adam has his reasons. It isn't any one thing that's driving him."

"You could change his mind. There're still months left before he needs to go."

"Maybe, but don't build your hopes on that. He's focused on what he wants."

"You can't let him, *Abba*." I wanted to cry.

"I can't stop him, Maya."

"Let me talk to him. If you can't keep him safe, then I will."

"No, Maya, don't."

"He's just a kid!" I slammed my fist on my desk. "He doesn't know shit yet. It's up to you to keep him safe—why won't you do that? He's your son!"

"Someone needs to defend Israel," he said. "If I won't let my son do it, how can I ask other people to let their sons go?"

"I don't care," I said. "Don't you think we've suffered enough? Haven't I suffered enough?"

He was silent for a moment.

"This isn't about you, Maya." He sounded tired and sad.

"It's about Adam. You can't take responsibility for everything that happens to the people you love."

I hung up and laid my head on my desk and cried. Would my loved ones never be safe?

That afternoon, in astronomy class, I signed up for all the night labs I could. If I couldn't sleep at night, I might as well spend those hours with a telescope.

Some nights I could catch a university bus to get to the observatory. The rest of the university would be left behind as the bus climbed the steep hill until it finally arrived at the observatory. It would stop short of the lab so its headlights wouldn't ruin the observers' night vision. Other nights I walked the whole way.

Those quiet nights, lit only by a dim red bulb, helped. No thoughts of war, no bloodshed. There was no guilt in a telescope, there were no accusations in the stars. Just cool blue light full of secrets and mysteries.

The observatory was a round little building, all red brick and climbing ivy. It had a silver dome that opened down the middle to let the telescope peer out. This was my ivory tower, and it was beautiful, serene, and safe.

Sometimes there were other students there and some nights I was there alone. It didn't matter to me. There was always the feeling of stillness and magical precision. The perfect balance of the telescope, thirty feet long, that could rotate with the lightest push seemed miraculous to me. To get to the eyepiece, I had to climb a narrow wooden ladder, then settle into the padded seat and stay there, hidden from sight, peeping in on celestial activities, taking notes.

Chris and I still went jogging twice a week, meeting at eight, finishing by a quarter to nine. I still hated running, but it always left me calm and steady for the night's work. He didn't talk as much about his girlfriend anymore. They had reached a decision during the vacation. He would go to Japan without her. They were free to date other people.

"It wasn't fair to keep pushing," he told me. "It wasn't the right sort of life for her."

He seemed more at ease now, and I was happy for him, but a little sad that their relationship hadn't worked out. With this newfound peace, however, he canceled more and more of our running dates. Too cold, too windy, too much work, and maybe, too many new girls to flirt with, though he never admitted that. He was right, of course; it was stupid to go out in the freezing cold when the gym was nearby, warm, well lit, with rows and rows of treadmills. But running on a treadmill, like a hamster on a wheel, just didn't give me the same release.

So I ran alone.

I hated running. I hated the burning in my lungs. I despised that rubbery feeling in my legs when I first started. It was even more hateful in the cold, in the dark, alone. But suffering proved I was alive. Pain spurred me on to run past it. And every once in a while, the misery faded, the pain disappeared, and there would be a moment of grace. In this moment, I didn't feel my legs at all, my breathing straightened out, and I was flying. In those crystal moments, time could stop and I could step outside everything. Remembering nothing. Just being. Feeling so light I floated above the ground, legs touching the earth merely out of habit.

It didn't always come, this out-of-body experience. I could never predict when it would. It was harder in the cold. With the metallic taste of blood in the back of my throat, my thighs itching with cold, my hands numb inside the gloves, it was much harder to leave all that behind.

Payton thought I was an idiot to run at night in the middle of winter. She told me so repeatedly. I wasn't an idiot. Just crazy and running to stay sane.

It was mid-February, and by now I felt I had the hang of cold-weather running. I ran without thinking about my stride, without thinking about my breathing. At ten degrees above freezing, it was downright balmy considering the past few weeks. There weren't many cars. I wasn't thinking about being careful, about watching my step. Arrogant and stupid.

I was thinking about Israel, about roasted eggplants and nearly burned pitas and a hundred other memories of warm sunshine and savory foods. Trying to decide if I should go home this summer or find a job in Charlottesville. Trying to decide what I could say to Adam to make him change his mind. Trying to understand why my father wasn't fighting him tooth and nail. *Ima* would be on my side. How could she not be?

I never noticed the small cluster of dried leaves on the curb. My foot skidded out. The momentum from the run and the slight twist of the turn pushed me into the street.

I slipped off the sidewalk and my ankle buckled from under me. I heard a distinct "pop" before falling heavily on my side and sprawling in the middle of the street.

I lay there for a moment, stunned. No pain yet, but a sick feeling in my stomach that it would come soon.

Shit.

I tried to sit up, and a wave of pain hit me so hard it made me nauseated.

"Fuck," I gasped out loud, upgrading my original assessment of the situation.

I had to get out of the road. I gingerly sat up and scooted over to the curb. The pain made me break out in a cold sweat. My ankle bumped up against the concrete and I could almost see colors in the wave of pain that rocked through me. My hip was sore from breaking my fall, and my elbow burned. The pavement had ripped through the sweatshirt. I was not surprised to see blood. I waited to catch my breath before daring to look at my ankle. It looked okay, not tilted at a crazy angle. No bones poking out of the skin. Good. But the longer I sat there, the more the pain grew.

"*L'Azazel*," I cursed in Hebrew. "*Kibinimat!*"

I don't know how long I sat on the curb before I saw car lights coming. I raised my head and watched it drive up, slow down, and stop in front of me.

The passenger-side window rolled down.

"Maya?" I heard. "Is that you? Are you okay?"

"No," I said. "I think my ankle is broken."

The driver-side door opened, and I watched someone get

out and walk toward me. The headlights were shining in my eyes and I couldn't see who it was.

He squatted in front of me.

"Jesus, Maya," Justin said, lightly touching the side of my face. I flinched. "What happened?"

"I fell."

"You're bleeding."

That explained why my face hurt too.

"I heard something pop," I said. Goose bumps crawled up my arms at the memory of that sound. "I think I need a doctor."

"Yeah," Justin said. "You do."

That's when I started to cry.

"Hey, now," he said. "Easy. We'll get you to the hospital, you'll be fine." His voice was calm and steady, but I could hear the fear behind it, and the fact that he was taking this so seriously made me realize what a mess I was in. "Can you stand?"

"No." I tried to stop crying. My chin wobbled with the effort.

He slipped one arm under my knees and the other around my back. He stood up, lifting me in one smooth motion. I held on to his neck and my tears left a damp smear on his sweater. As he placed me in the car, my ankle bumped against the door. I tried not to scream.

"You're doing great," he said.

"I'm fine," I lied. "I'm just glad you found me." Which was probably the truest thing I'd ever said.

He got in the car and put it in gear. I could feel him looking at me.

"Don't fall asleep," he said when I closed my eyes. "I don't think you should fall asleep."

"I don't have a concussion. My hip broke most of the fall."

"Don't say 'broke' and 'hip' in the same sentence, okay?" I almost giggled. "How the hell did you do this to yourself?" He almost sounded mad.

"I slipped," I said. "Gravity took over. You know, momentum. Inertia. Newton's Laws."

"Very funny."

"I didn't think so at the time. I still don't."

Justin pulled up at the emergency-room entrance and left me in the idling car. He came back minutes later with a nurse and a wheelchair.

The two of them eased me out of the car and into the wheelchair. I was off, wheeling along into the fluorescent lights of the emergency room, shaky again in the aftermath of being moved. Keeping my whole leg still, that was clearly the answer. Moving was bad. I decided I was not getting out of that wheelchair. Ever.

"I'll be right back," Justin said, squeezing my hand. "I have a buddy in ortho who works here. I'm going to go find him."

The nurse handed me a clipboard and I started filling in my information. Address. Allergies. Medication. Insurance. I didn't have any ID on me. Only the key to my room. I managed to borrow a phone. I called Payton and left a message on our machine asking her to come by the hospital with my backpack.

Half an hour went by. I was promised some X-rays.

Another half hour went by and I was wheeled to another room. The X-rays were taken and I was wheeled back out to the waiting room. I was still waiting for Justin to come back. Where was Payton? It was a weeknight, for heaven's sake—what was she doing out so late?

We were a sad, quiet group in the waiting room, sorry beings waiting to be helped at ten at night. There were at least two moms with kids bundled up in blankets and coughing miserably. I eyed an elderly man in the corner who didn't seem to have an obvious problem and a man in his late thirties cradling his right arm.

My battered face drew some looks, and I wondered if Justin would get questioned. Man brings in bruised and bleeding woman, claiming she fell. Classic story, right? I didn't know whether to be concerned or amused that bringing me in might land him in a spot of trouble.

Payton arrived with my backpack.

"Oh my God," she gasped. She kneeled by the wheelchair and touched my hair lightly.

"That bad?" I said, trying to be funny.

"You look a lot worse than you sounded on the phone."

"I haven't seen a mirror. I guess they don't keep one around here on purpose."

"Oh, Maya, I didn't mean it like that." Her hands fluttered helplessly and then settled down at her sides. I could tell she wanted to hug me, but all things considered it was probably best if she didn't. Everything hurt, even my skin. "What happened?"

I shrugged, then winced. "I was running and I fell and something went pop." I still couldn't get over the fact I heard my own bone snapping. "My ankle's broken, I think. Then Justin drove by and he saw me. He brought me here."

"And then he left you?" Payton's voice rose in alarm.

"No, no. He went to find some doctor he knows." I looked over at the hallway I'd last seen him walk down. "I don't know where he is, though. It's been a while since he left."

"Oh." Then she opened her mouth and I braced myself for what I saw coming. "I told you it was dangerous to go running alone. What if Justin hadn't come by?"

"I'm lucky he did."

"Jesus, Maya!" She noticed my face and her anger deflated. "Oh, listen to me, yelling at you in a hospital. I'm sorry. Do you need me to call anyone? Your parents?"

"No, don't do that. Let me wait until I see a doctor and find out what's wrong before I talk to them."

"But your dad's a doctor, he might be able to help."

"Payton," I said. "My dad's an optometrist. I broke my ankle. I don't see how he could help."

"You're right. Absolutely. Okay. What can I get you? Do you want some Tylenol? I've got some in my purse. Or something to drink? A soda?"

"No, I'm fine." I didn't feel fine, but Payton was starting to panic. "Why don't you go look for Justin? I haven't seen him since we got here. He said his friend was in ortho—maybe you could ask someone where that is."

"Okay, sure. I'll find him and bring him back." She turned

to leave, then returned to me again. "Are you sure you'll be okay alone?"

"Pay, I'm in a hospital."

"Right. Okay. I'll go find Justin."

"Great. Thanks."

While Justin was gone tracking down his elusive friend and Payton was gone tracking down Justin, I sat alone, surrounded by strangers, in pain. I should have been scared. But I was actually calm and felt somewhat detached from the moment. I wasn't going to be able to run away from this.

I was thinking that this was a funny way to be feeling, and that maybe I had hit my head harder than I thought, when a nurse escorted Yami to one of the empty chairs.

"Please remain seated," the nurse said. "A doctor will be with you shortly."

Yami nodded mutely and slumped uneasily in the bucket seat.

I wondered if I should say something. But I was too far away to get her attention without yelling. I debated whether she wanted to be left alone. Maybe she wouldn't appreciate seeing me. But she looked forlorn and scared. With a bit of difficulty and a few bolts of pain from my hip and elbow, I managed to get the chair moving and inched up to her.

Yami looked up as I wheeled near her. She sat up and several emotions flashed across her face before settling into lines of concern.

"What happened to you?"

"I fell."

"Out of your dorm room?" The horror on her face startled a laugh out of me.

"No. I'd look a hell of a lot worse than this if I did that. I fell while running. I think I broke something. What's your story?"

She looked away and I wondered if I wasn't supposed to ask.

"I couldn't breathe." She touched her throat. "I was just lying there in bed and I felt like someone was pressing a pillow to my face. Like in those stupid murder mysteries. It just wouldn't go away. Maybe I'm having an asthma attack or a heart attack."

"Did you come here alone?"

"I called a taxi."

"Do you want me to call someone to come get you after the doctor sees you?" It upset me to think of her in fear of her life, coming here alone, waiting to be seen alone, going back to an empty house. Alone.

"Don't bother," she said. "I'm probably fine. It's no big deal."

"Two of my friends are here. One of them could take you home. Maybe you shouldn't be home alone tonight."

"Don't bother," she said again. "I'm fine."

Then Justin came in, smiling, leading a tired resident who looked like he'd just been pulled out of bed. Which, as it turned out, is exactly what had happened. Payton was a few steps behind them, smiling tentatively.

"Time to see the good doctor," Justin said. He grabbed my wheelchair and started wheeling me out of the waiting room.

"Wait, what's your cell-phone number?" I made him write

it down and handed it to Yami. "Good luck. Call if you need help getting home."

She took the number and nodded, but I could tell she wasn't going to call.

"Who was that?" Justin asked as we left the waiting room.

"That's the woman who cleans our dorm," Payton said, looking over her shoulder at Yami. "She doesn't look so good."

"She might need help getting home," I said.

"Let's deal with getting you home for now," Justin said, wheeling me toward a long hallway.

"Okay," I said. I was suddenly nervous with a doctor nearby. "Let's get this over with."

It was very late by the time Justin and Pay were helping me up the stairs to my dorm room.

"This is going to be fun," I said. "Two flights of stairs on crutches for the next four weeks."

"As Confucius says—a journey of a thousand miles begins with a single step."

I rolled my eyes at Justin's weak attempt at humor.

"You're stronger than you think," Payton said, her new personal mantra. "You can do this."

They each held one of my crutches and had an arm around my waist. My left arm was over Justin's shoulder and my right was over Payton's, and their height difference made it awkwardly lopsided.

Sweat beaded between my shoulder blades and I fought

down nausea rising from the effort, the painkillers, and the lack of sleep.

I stopped on the landing between the two floors.

"Give me a minute."

"I could just carry you," Justin offered again.

"No." I swallowed. "I'll give you a hernia and then we'll have to go back to the emergency room." My face was hot. My hands were icy cold.

"God, you're stubborn."

"Just give me a minute."

The three of us stood there while I fought off a cold sweat and rolling waves of dizzy queasiness.

"Forget this," Justin said. He handed his crutch to Payton and swung me up in a cradle carry.

"Oh God, no." My world tilted and the nausea clicked higher. I clung on, nearly choking him. "I can't do this."

He took the stairs two at a time and I felt the pressure ride up the back of my throat. We reached my hallway and he headed toward my room, with Payton hurrying after us.

"Bathroom," I managed to croak before the gagging started.

He caught the look on my face and grimly headed to the women's bathroom. He walked straight to the toilets and set me down gently so I half lay, half sprawled against the commode.

"Oh God," I moaned, feeling very sorry for myself, and heaved into the pot.

* * *

"You're okay now."

I felt a cold washcloth on my face. I kept my eyes closed.

"I called Jonah. He said to go easy on you. He said you should eat something next time you take the ibuprofen . . . I didn't mean to make you sick."

I kept my eyes closed but smiled despite myself.

"She lives," he said. "I saw that."

I opened my eyes. He was sitting on the edge of my bed, looking as tired and scraggly as I felt. I patted his hand.

"No worries." My voice sounded raspy. "I feel much better now."

It was true. I was floating softly on a wave of painkillers, an empty stomach, and the end of a long, adrenaline-filled day. With my eyes closed, I only saw a soft darkness; there were none of the usual swirling colors and shapes that normally live on the inside of my eyelids.

"Where's Payton?"

"She went to get Yami from the hospital."

I tried to think about that. About what that meant. I was alone with Justin.

"Tell me a story," I said. "Until I fall asleep. Give me something nice to think about."

"A story?" I had surprised him. "Hmm, let me think about this." He shifted uncomfortably on the edge of my bed. "Can you scoot over a bit?"

I shifted so that I lay at the very edge of my bed, wedged in against the wall. He readjusted the pillow that my leg was propped on so that it supported my ankle properly. Then he settled down, back against the headboard, long legs stretched out next to me. My head rested near his hip. We were both quiet for a moment while he thought about his story.

This was the closest I'd been to him since the night we'd slept together. This was the longest we'd been together since then. If I moved my fingers just a little bit, they would touch his thigh, but I didn't move. When he started talking, his voice sounded like it was coming from far away.

"My brothers and I would sneak out at night sometimes to look at the stars." He spoke quietly, trying to lull me to sleep. I heard the soft hum of the heaters, steady and dull, as he spun a web around us. "We'd go to our backyard and stretch out, a lot like this, and tell each other stories about how the stars got where they were. My older brother, Cooper, would tell the most amazing stories, about kings and evil warriors. He would create and destroy empires and swear it was all true."

He fell silent. I kept my eyes closed and tried only to picture what he was saying. I could see them, three blond boys outside late at night.

"I guess he learned about the constellations at school, and he liked to read a lot. So he would mix the stories up and invent stuff and then leave his story in the sky for me to think about.

"I remember how when we would go back inside, I could never stop thinking about the stories he told and I would look at the stars from my bed and not be able to sleep." His voice was disembodied and floating toward me. "The next day, I would be exhausted and my mother would yell at my brothers to leave me alone. I was always worried they would listen to her and not wake me up next time they went outside, but they always did. Cooper made me love the stars. Made me see how special they were. I can understand why you love them."

I wondered how he knew that. I wondered if he was trying to break my heart. I was still trying to decide that when I fell asleep.

When I woke up, he was gone. Payton was in the room, quietly working at her desk.

"Hey." I struggled to sit up. "You're back."

"You're awake! I was starting to worry."

"What time is it?" My voice was raspy and I cleared my throat.

Payton came over, sat on my bed, and glanced at her watch. "Almost one."

"Wow. Late."

"Yeah," she said softly. "How are you feeling?"

"Like I was run over by a truck."

"You look like it too."

"Great." I didn't want to ask about Justin, but she saw my look and grinned.

"He only left about an hour ago," she said. "In case you were wondering where he was."

I shrugged as if to say, "Who, me?"

"He was so sweet," she said, not falling for it. "He kept reminding me to make sure you eat something before you take your anti-inflammatory pills."

I winced at the memory of what happened last night when I didn't eat before taking the pills.

"We're friends," I said to Payton, trying to stop the eyebrow-waggling and significant looks she kept sending my way. I'd overheard a girl in the cafeteria say that once. I remember thinking it was such a lame thing to say. Look at me now.

"Sure," Payton said. Despite looking like a sweet cheerleader, she had not, in fact, been born yesterday.

"Did Justin say that Yami called last night?" It seemed like a good idea to change the topic.

"No, she didn't call. But Justin seemed to have things under control." She gave me another look. I ignored it. "He said I could use his car, so I figured I'd stop by the ER and see if she was still there."

"How was she?"

"She was fine. They couldn't find anything wrong. I think they gave her a Valium or something. They were really patronizing."

"But she's okay, right? What did she say when you showed up?"

Payton snorted. "She was pretty surprised. And yeah, I mean, I guess she's okay. I drove her to her apartment."

I shifted and scooted up on the bed to a sitting position. Payton fixed the pillow under my leg.

"I don't know, Maya," she said, shrugging uncomfortably. "It was one of the saddest things I've ever seen. She was all relaxed from the drugs and she started talking as I was driving. Did you know she had a son?"

I shook my head.

"He died five years ago. He was just three years old. Can you imagine that? It was some stupid drunk driver."

"Oh." I had an uncomfortable feeling that this made sense. That the reason Yami could talk to me was because of that. We understood what it meant to stand at the edge of a precipice and then reluctantly step away, leaving someone precious behind.

"She was driving and this car just slams into them. You should have heard her when she was telling me. I almost started crying."

I was in bed with morning breath, greasy hair (I never did shower after my run), and aches and pains that were returning with a vengeance. I was starting to regret ever mentioning anything. I didn't want to know any more.

"She thinks it was her fault. After all these years, she's still punishing herself. It's like after her son died, she never wanted to be close to anyone ever again. Never wanted to care about anything or anyone. Imagine being sick enough to need an emergency room and to be there alone. But I think she wanted it that way."

I tried not to flinch. I wondered if it was Yami she was talking about.

"Now, then," she said, rising from my bed. "What can I get you to drink? The fridge is stocked. Diet Coke, orange juice, iced tea? You name it and chances are we've got it."

"Iced tea," I said. "In a glass, not a bottle."

"Coming right up."

Was Payton right? Last night, as I waited for Justin and

Payton in the emergency room, I'd realized that somehow, despite myself, I had made good friends. Friends who took care of me, whom I would protect, even though I was still scared to admit I truly cared for them. Yami lived life without anyone to love, without anything to lose. No job she cared about, no friends or lovers. She lived the life I thought I wanted. And yet all I felt for her was pity.

The next day, I called Justin. He'd called me twice and stopped by when I wasn't in. I knew if I didn't get back to him soon my behavior would cross into unpardonably rude and pathetically cowardly. So I took a deep breath and dialed.

"It's me," I said.

"Alive?"

"Yeah. Sorry I didn't call sooner."

There was a pause, and I hated the fact that I was sitting alone in my room, clutching the phone and feeling like a complete idiot.

"I haven't thanked you for everything you did for me. I don't know what I would have done if you hadn't come when you did." I heard him take a breath to answer and I rushed on. "Let me take you out to lunch, it's the least I can do."

"Okay."

"Good. That's great."

"Where?" His one-word answers were starting to annoy me.

"What?"

"Where do you want to meet for lunch? What time?"

I started to answer, then stopped. My heart was racing, my mouth was dry. Stupid, I thought to myself. It's different here. Be an adult. But this reminded me so much of my conversation with Dov that it made me feel a little sick. I felt that cold rush of adrenaline making my hands shake.

"It doesn't matter to me," I managed to say. "Just pick a place."

"You're paying," he said. "You pick."

"It doesn't matter!" He was silent. "Fine, how about Star Hill Café?" I named a nearby place. "But you say when."

"I'm free any day after eleven, so it doesn't matter to me."

"It does!" My voice sounded shrill and my knuckles had turned white where I was clutching the desk. Even I could see I was being ridiculous. I took a deep breath. "This is so hard," I said. "I know this sounds strange to you, but I can't pick the time. I just can't do it."

There was silence on the line and I would have given a lot to know what he was thinking, the look on his face.

"I'm not sure what this is about," he said slowly, the way you would talk to a man brandishing a knife. "You're almost as upset about this as you were about your ankle." He stopped. I held my breath. "This has something to do with your past, in Israel," he said.

I felt my stomach twist, and I swallowed, trying to get rid of a bitterness that suddenly filled me. That's the problem with having a professional student care for you—you're studied, compared, contrasted, and certain conclusions are drawn.

I thought about denying it. I thought about hanging up.

But instead I sat up and, with my heart hammering, I didn't run away.

"Yes," I said. My voice was low and husky but steady, and it strengthened me. "I'll tell you about it. But not on the phone. Meet me today. At one-thirty."

And just like that, I made plans.

We met for lunch, and while I couldn't help but eye people's backpacks and one shifty-looking businessman, I did manage to order lunch and enjoy my portobello mushroom sandwich and roasted-bell-pepper soup. I had picked a late lunch on purpose so that the café was more than half empty. It was cold and gray outside, and the café was bright and warm and cozy. I'd draped my jacket on the back of my chair but left my soft blue scarf around my neck like a safety blanket. We talked for a while about my ankle and getting used to crutches. My arms were sore from the effort. Justin told a funny story about envying his brother's broken leg and crutches and trying to break his own leg in third grade. Fortunately he failed; unfortunately his mother found out.

"I was grounded for two weeks," he said. "Not only didn't I have the cool cast and the crutches, I didn't even get to watch TV or eat any dessert."

I laughed.

He smiled and shrugged. "That's how life goes, you don't always get what you want."

"And sometimes you want things that it's better you didn't get in the first place."

"That too."

I took a deep breath and plunged in.

"A year ago I applied to UVA, and when I was accepted, I wasn't sure what to do." I stared at my half-eaten sandwich and the empty cup of soup stained red from the peppers. "I had a boyfriend—his name was Dov. And I loved him." I met Justin's eyes. "I loved him very much."

He nodded. The words were coming easily, much more easily than I'd expected. Now that I'd decided to tell him, everything was rushing out. I had to make an effort to slow down, to speak coherently.

"I wanted to come here very badly, but I also loved Dov and I didn't want to be away for four years. I thought if I left then, we would break up—and I didn't want that. So I was very unhappy. I couldn't decide. Which one, right? All the excitement and adventure of coming to another country, or staying in my homeland with my family and my friends and Dov."

I stopped, because this was the hard part. The part where everything went wrong. I felt Justin's gaze on me. Justin Case, who had rescued me, who had made love to me, who waited now with more patience and kindness than I would ever have imagined.

"But finally I made my decision. I decided I would come here and that if Dov really loved me, he would let me, and we would make it work. I would go home every summer, he would visit me here. . . . I told him to meet me at my favorite café because I wanted to tell him face to face, not on the phone." I felt hot tears make their way slowly down my face. I let them fall and kept talking. "There was a bomb." I closed my eyes. "A suicide bomber. A waiter who used to work there. I was the one who got him fired and after that he never got another job. For almost a year he was unemployed and his bitterness just grew and grew. I wasn't even there, I was running late. Isn't that a joke? I was on the bus and I even heard the explosion and I had no idea I had just killed my boyfriend."

Justin grabbed my hand and squeezed it hard.

"You didn't kill him," he said fiercely, and gave me a little shake. "That bomber killed him."

"If I hadn't gotten him fired, if I hadn't told Dov to meet me there, it would never have happened."

"Yeah, you're right," he said. I looked up from my lap because no one had ever said that before. "If you hadn't existed, then maybe this wouldn't have happened. But whatever that waiter did to get himself fired would have probably happened sooner or later with someone else. You can't live life hoping nothing you do affects anything or anyone else. That's just life. You can't predict how the most simple thing will turn out, but that doesn't mean that you step away from living life and try to hide away."

People were staring at us, and realizing he was nearly shouting, Justin let go of my hand and leaned back in his chair.

"It wasn't wrong of you to want to talk to your boyfriend face to face, just like it wasn't wrong of you to want to tell me this face to face. It wasn't wrong of you to get some crazy waiter fired. It is awful that he became a suicide bomber. It is terrible that your boyfriend was killed. But you are not responsible for either of those events. There is one person who is. And he's dead."

I blew my nose.

"Maya," he said. "Look at me."

I met his gaze.

"Accidents of timing happen everywhere. You ask someone to come over and they get hit by a car on the way. Does that mean you shouldn't have asked them over? Does that mean you shouldn't have any friends on the off chance they'll get hurt? You can't live like that. No one can. You just have to accept that. There's no point to life if you take away all the beauty of friendships and love." He grabbed both my hands, and his hands were so warm against mine. "So many things make sense now," he said. "The way you behaved after you spent the night with me. Why you were always so distant with the other students in class. You tried to build a mile-high wall around yourself. But don't you see, even when you tried not to care for anyone, you did."

I sniffed. I didn't know what to say.

"I need to go wash my face." I stood up, got my crutches, and made my way to the restrooms in the rear of the café. Once inside, I took a shaky breath and splashed cold water on my red face. It was the first time I'd talked about Dov, about what happened, since I'd left Israel. It hurt, but in a strange way it felt good. I was glad Justin knew what happened, that he didn't pull away in horror, that he didn't think less of me. I realized I had also come close to apologizing for the things I'd said after we'd slept together. That was good. He deserved a real explanation.

I studied myself in the mirror. I saw a red-eyed girl who looked tired but peaceful and calm. I smiled at her.

"You've been gone a long time," I told her. "Welcome back."

The cast stayed on for four long, foul weeks, but I was determined to keep going to the observatory almost every night.

Payton came with me once, and even though I got her to admit that the building was beautiful and the telescope was amazing, on our ride home she shook her head.

"Aren't you afraid?" she asked. "All alone, surrounded by a forest. It's so dark there, and creepy. Anyone could be hiding out."

I tried to explain, but she didn't get it.

After I learned how to operate the telescope, I volunteered to help the graduate students with the night labs. The professor gave me a key and I would touch it during the day, running my fingers over its ridges. I couldn't get over the fact that they trusted me with a key to the observatory. I seized any excuse to go there, and after a while I stopped needing official reasons and just went for reasons of my own.

I loved climbing that narrow wooden ladder (I'd leave my crutches leaning against the railing and hop up the stairs, one at a time). I loved settling into the padded seat and staying there, hidden from sight, my eye trained on points of light universes away.

* * *

I met Justin for lunch a couple of times a week. We talked a lot about philosophy and justice and blame. I was not the first mortal to ponder such things. I was amazed by what Justin had studied and how relevant debates from three thousand years ago still were today. The nature of good and evil, one man's responsibility to his brother. I was especially taken by the words of Epictetus, a Roman slave from two thousand years ago. His advice: let go of what you cannot control, focus only on what falls directly under your control—your opinions, your will, your moral fortitude. I tried to follow that advice.

When I'd finally gotten used to walking around on crutches, it was time for the cast to come off. I needed to go to physical therapy to learn to walk again. Four weeks, apparently, was long enough for a person who'd been walking for twenty years to forget how to do it properly. My foot would come down flat, as if still bound in a cast, so I looked like I was limping or at least walking on the deck of a rolling ship, even though the ground was flat and the cast was off.

"It's not serious," the physical therapist laughed when I expressed my concern. "Your muscles have adapted to one situation, and you just need to remind them to go back to the way things used to be. Your muscles retain the memory of walking right." She rotated my ankle, then rolled my foot in a pantomime of a footstep. "It's like my kids going back to school after summer vacation. They just need a review of what they learned last year."

She showed me a photocopied sheet of ankle exercises and gave me stretchy bands in two colors of resistance.

"You'll be walking normally in a few days," she said as she signed my chart. "But keep up the exercises for another three weeks. You need to keep building up the muscles around your ankle to stabilize it and protect it, like a built-in ankle brace."

She was right. Within a day, I no longer walked funny. By the next day, I didn't even need to think about rolling my foot and coming off the balls of my feet as I walked. The memory of walking returned to my foot, just like she said it would.

The orthopedist and the physical therapist said I could start running again. Not for miles, because my muscles had atrophied, but for as long as I was able to run comfortably. A week had passed and I hadn't gone. Not yet. I believed you should walk before you run, and besides, it was running that had gotten me into this mess in the first place. I was a little hesitant to go at it again, but that left me with no outlet. No true solitude. No escape from this body.

A week after I learned to walk again, it started to snow.

When I had come up to the observatory that night, I knew I would not get any work done, not with a heavy cloud cover and the weatherman excitedly calling for five inches, unusual this late in the year. But I had come up anyway, planning to work on the computers up there and get some homework done.

After pulling away from the distractions during the day and sleeping until noon, I rode to the lab. As I got off the shuttle, the driver warned me that he might not be able to get back up the mountain to get me.

"If it starts snowing like they say it will, there's no way I could get this thing up here. And they won't clear the snow off O-Hill until tomorrow at the earliest."

"That's okay," I said. "If it snows, I'll just walk back." I wiggled my foot, still pleased I could wear shoes and that I didn't need crutches.

"I don't recommend it," he said. "It's a long walk, and it'll be cold and slippery."

"I know."

"Look, I can't be responsible—"

"You're not. I am. Thanks for the ride."

I got out of the van before he could say anything else. He grumbled under his breath and then pulled away. I watched him go with an odd feeling of satisfaction.

As I let myself in and waited for the lights to stop blinking and stay on, I could see how someone might find it creepy. Alone, on top of a hill, with a snowstorm coming. But it wasn't creepy to me. It was wonderful.

I booted up one of the computers and flicked on the electric kettle. I made a cup of instant coffee, turned it creamy with powder, and settled down in front of the computer.

The door opened a few hours later. I saved my work and got up to see who had come.

I was taken aback as he took off his heavy coat and rubbed his hands briskly.

"What are you doing here?" I asked.

Justin looked up. His gray eyes were so clear that they reminded me of rain puddles when the skies clear and the sun shines again.

"I came looking for you," he said. Then he turned and carefully shut the door behind him.

He looked around, taking in the large photographs of the Horseshoe Nebula, the silver craters of the moon, a spiral galaxy. They had become so familiar to me I hardly saw them. I looked at them again now. We stood side by side in silence, once again the only two people in the world awake so late at night. It was past midnight. I wondered if he couldn't sleep. I wondered why he'd come.

"Did Payton tell you where I was?"

"Yes. Do you mind?"

"No," I said. "Do you want me to show you around?"

"Of course."

I wondered if Payton had called him because she was worried about me getting stuck here in the snow. It would be like her.

We walked into the dome and I showed him the telescope, the reading instruments, and pointed out the pulleys and gears used to turn this graceful beast. I spoke softly, my voice low, my accent softer than usual. He listened quietly, and I felt that perhaps we were the only two people in the world.

"It's cloudy out and about to snow, otherwise I'd show you the stars." I smiled because it sounded like a pickup line. He didn't smile back.

"You remind me of a medieval monk, hiding out in your

sanctuary on top of a mountain, removed from society, sheltered from life."

"I wish I could live here," I said. "I would if I could."

I knew he thought this was a bad thing, that I was still scared of being a part of life, but he was wrong. I wished I could show him the rings of Saturn or the icy moons of Jupiter, or the gas nebula in Orion's Belt. But clouds had covered every inch of sky and there was nothing to see through the telescope but gray cotton. He joined me in the computer lab, a small cream-colored room with more photographs, mostly from the Hubble Telescope.

"I brought work with me," he said. "I'll stay until you're ready to leave."

He unzipped his bag and took out his papers. We settled in to work in silence. Every so often I could feel him looking up from his work and glancing at me. I refused to look at him. I stared straight at my computer, typing. I couldn't remember why I was so afraid of falling in love with him. At half past two I gave a big stretch. He yawned. We smiled.

"You about ready to give up?" he asked.

"Yes," I said. "I'm done."

We gathered our things, and I began the long process of dressing to go outside. On came the sweater, the scarf, the thick wool coat, the gloves, and the fleece-lined hat.

"You look like you're going out to do battle," he laughed.

"I am. I hate the cold. Between me and the cold, it's war."

"At least you're guaranteed victory. In two months the war will be over and you'll have won."

I smiled.

I couldn't believe I'd ever longed for snow, for frost to settle on the ground. Now that it was here, I couldn't stand it. He shrugged into his jacket, clearly at ease with the thought of heading out with a bare head and a neck vulnerable to any passing gust.

"Can I walk you home?"

While we had been inside studying, the snow had started, and now everywhere, everything was coated in white. All the edges in the world had been erased. Everything was soft and out of focus, and even though it was night, the land glowed.

I should have known that looks were deceiving. We had been walking in silent companionship for nearly half an hour. We'd already come down Observatory Hill and had entered the main body of the university, our steps muffled by thousands of tiny white flakes. The next thing I knew, my feet shot out from under me. I was suspended in midair for a moment before I came crashing down. There was ringing in my head. I could hear the trees laughing.

"Are you all right?" he choked out.

It wasn't the trees I heard laughing.

"This is not funny," I said, grumpy and embarrassed. "Not funny at all. I could have broken my ankle again."

He didn't hear me. He couldn't hear me. He was howling with laughter. He said something that sounded like "The look on your face . . ." and then "Sorry" and "Sorry" again. But each time he tried to speak, he only laughed harder. I struggled to my feet, disgusted with him and myself. The snow was sticking to my jacket and pants, coating them in white.

He rushed to help me up.

"Oh, stop it." I pushed at him and fell down again. He looked like he wanted to laugh again, but this time, valuing his life, he took some deep breaths instead.

"Are you all right?" he asked, his lips barely twitching at all. "Is your ankle okay?"

"I'm fine." I sat up.

After a moment of hesitation he lay down next to me, stretched out on his back, arms pillowing his head. I paused, looked at him, and then I lay back down too. From where we lay, looking at the sky, the snow was madly swirling. Snowflakes landed in the corner of my eye and on my eyelashes.

Later, when I was back in my room, I would look in horror at my fingers and toes, seeing them with a blue tint for the first time in my life. But then, lying in the snow, I didn't feel the cold at all.

"Better?" Justin asked after a moment.

"Yes." The ache in my back was beginning to fade and my ankle wasn't hurting. Wetness was starting to seep in through my jeans, but I didn't move.

I looked at him lying next to me, Nordic skin only a little flushed, and I knew we were different to our cores. My olive skin didn't know what to do about this cold. I had never seen so much snow in my life. Israel seemed as far away as a dream.

"In the Negev Desert sometimes the sky seems white,

there are so many stars. Like snow." For the first time in months, I could think of something beautiful from home without a stab of pain. "The first time my friends and I went hiking there, we walked thirty kilometers in one day, and when we finally stopped for the night, I was so exhausted that I couldn't think of anything but sleep." My face was numb and it was hard to talk. Snow kept falling in my eyes, so I closed them.

"People were telling stories around the fire and I was fighting sleep, trying to remember everything they said because it was so funny and I wanted to tell my brother when I got back. But when we finally all stretched out in our tents, I couldn't fall asleep. I was too hot, closed in. The breathing of other people irritated me." I shifted with the memory of it. I had to make him understand. I had to make him know who I was. Who I used to be. "I crawled out and dragged my sleeping bag with me and found a spot a little apart from the tents. The wind was blowing and I could hear the rustle of the sand and tiny animals. I just sat there and looked at the stars and realized this was where I was supposed to be.

"There were so many stars they kept me awake. It was hard to find the Big Dipper, that's how many stars there were. The Milky Way was a huge bright stain. I'd never seen anything like it. I never have since then."

The sky I was looking at now was bright. I was encircled by glowing snow and light, and only the area between sky and earth was in dark shadow, and even it was speckled with thousands and thousands of tiny silver flakes. We were in a distant corner of the campus and I wondered if I would ever find it again. That place must have been enchanted.

"There were not many times when I understood why the land of Israel is important to us, why we keep fighting for it, year after year," I whispered. "But that night, looking at all those stars, knowing they were so far, millions and millions of light years away, but still we can see them, that's when I knew why we keep fighting. We do it because after each war, after each victory and every death, we keep thinking and hoping it will be over." I was frozen. An ice maiden. I could review my life floating above it all, no recriminations, no regrets, no tears.

"Even though peace is so far away, light years away, on some nights, when everything is quiet and we are with friends," I touched his hand, "we can see peace in the distance."

I realized I truly believed that. It made me glad.

"The old Bedouin who was our guide was also out there," I said. "He said men get drunk from the night sky of the Negev. He said there is no place on earth like the Negev on a clear night." I remembered how he smoked a pipe and the smoke wrapped around him like mist. "He had been offered a job in the city, he told me. But he would never leave the Negev. He said he would never leave it for a job in the city."

We lay side by side with snow swirling around us. My beloved stars, the light in the distance, united us. Talking became harder as my face went numb. The snow beneath me had now melted, soaking my legs and back. We lay side by side and did not touch until finally he said we should get up. He slowly stood and then helped me, his arms around my waist and shoulder to keep me steady and stop me from falling. More than anything we had done before, this was close to love.

It was hard to recognize him through the film of crystals on his face and hair. A drop of icy water glided down my back, and I shivered with the painful chill of it. He walked me home and snow continued to drift. I pictured the twin tracks of footprints we left behind us, slowly disappearing under new snow, and I knew they were proof we were there.

I had to keep my teeth clenched to stop them from chattering. But for the first time in so long, I felt good and clean. My soul renewed. I did not know how to thank him for this gift.

When we reached my building, I thanked him for walking with me. He didn't speak for a moment, his breath forming a cloud around his face. Snow eddied around him like a cloak.

"Will you stay here?" he asked. I knew what he wanted to know.

"Maybe," I said. "I don't know."

He nodded as if I'd said what he expected to hear.

"Call me when you go up to the observatory next time. I'll walk you home."

My face was frozen. I could barely speak.

"Thank you," I managed. "I will."

Then I caught his hand before he could turn away. I held his warm hand to my frozen cheek and I closed my eyes.

He leaned in and brushed his lips across mine.

I met his gaze and I smiled.

"*Ani ohevet otcha*," I said very softly.

"I love you too, Greenland," he said. "I have for months."

I was embarrassed and surprised that he knew what I had said.

He smiled. "It's amazing what you can learn on the Internet."

I laughed out loud and hugged him. He hugged me back, a huge bear hug, squeezing me through all those layers of Gore-Tex and fleece and cotton.

Then he walked off into the snow, leaving a path of footsteps behind him. I climbed the stairs to my room, leaving a trail of melted snow, achingly wishing for blue skies and yellow dunes.

After that night, I slept again.

The garden was beautifully kept, with perfectly trimmed hedges. April brought blooming flowers so thick they looked like pillows, and a lawn as smooth as carpet. This was where my lovers had come. Where I still came when I wanted to be alone. But like them, I discovered this garden was not as private as it seemed.

I had come to the garden the week before. I had just finished a long night lab, rushed home, written a paper, and then run to class to hand it in to the professor. Walking home, I was so tired that as I passed the garden, I couldn't resist that lazy sun that sapped my strength or that smooth expanse of grass. I stretched out on the soft lawn and fell asleep.

I woke up feeling funny. I sat up to find that a drawing class had come to the gardens to sketch. One of the students who entered my garden had set up her easel several feet in front of me. She was busy sketching when I sat up. We both looked at each other in surprise. Running a hand through my disheveled hair, I grabbed my jacket and backpack and fled.

I wondered if I would ever find a sketch of myself, sleeping, at some student art show on campus. If I did, I would ask to buy it and I would hang it in my room and call it "Healed."

The year was almost over. I had already taken all my finals but one. Summer was nearly here. I could feel the weight of the heat building each day, the growing press of humidity that curled my hair and drew beads of sweat from my skin like a snake charmer.

I lay on the itchy grass now and watched the busy life of ants and little black insects among their skyscraper blades of grass. They seemed frantic to me, hurrying everywhere they went, their short lives filled with work, danger, and the struggle to find food.

And my short life? Probably similar to theirs, if astronomy could be compared to digging tunnels and bringing home crumbs, and if politics and suicide bombers were similar to the heavy tread of uncaring humans and the sharp teeth of crickets.

My birthday was in two days. I was going to be twenty-one. Legally allowed to drink alcohol in Virginia. Payton was very excited. I had a ticket to fly home the week after that. Most of my stuff would stay at Payton's house for the summer, and I'd pick it up when I returned. We were going to be roommates next year. In a real apartment. With a kitchen. I was looking forward to traveling without so many bags.

Summer in Israel. Payton is talking about visiting, against her parents' wishes. They think it's too dangerous. But I want her to come. I want to show her the Mediterranean. I want her to taste our amazing produce, nothing like the watery tomatoes and bitter cucumbers found here. I want her to float in the Dead Sea, to climb to the top of Masada, to see the Roman ruins in Caesarea, the Dome of the Rock, the Western Wall. I want her to see our orchards and our skyscrapers. I want to take her to dance clubs in Tel Aviv and the white beaches of Haifa. I want her to fall in love with Israel and find it swimming in her blood the way I do.

I want Justin to come. I want to show him the real meaning of history. The burned-out truck shells that still line the road to Jerusalem from the siege in 1948. I want him to look for Roman coins on the beach, because you can still find them, if you're lucky. I want him to see the Turkish influence in Acre, a port Napoleon failed to breach. I want him to see the Knights' Hall there and the little Arab boys that jump off the parapets into the turquoise waters of the Mediterranean. I want to take him to the village of al-Qantir that was founded by Seti, father of Ramses II, around 1300 BCE. I want to take him camping in the Judean Desert.

I don't want to listen to the news.

I want to go home.

I am not afraid anymore. I am only homesick. And I smile, stretched out in Jefferson's garden with a hot Virginia sun beaming down.

Because I'm going home.

ACKNOWLEDGMENTS

Saying that something is "a dream come true" can be such a cliché, but of course clichés come about because sometimes they capture the essence of a situation. Publishing a novel has always been my dream, and with this book, my dream has come true. As always, no one achieves her dreams alone. It is only with the help, support, and expert knowledge of many people that I am here, living the cliché.

Thank you to my agents, Andrea Somberg and Donald Maass, and my editor, Erin Clarke, who made this experience wonderful and a whole lot of fun.

Thank you to Israeli Defense Force soldiers Shira Kravitz, Sally Maron, Hilla Revell, and Edo Schaefer. Your courage, your humor, and your adventures prove that fiction pales in comparison to life.

Thank you to dear friends Denise Grolly-Case and Sarah Leffler, whose loud and cheerful encouragement gave me the courage to continue.

Thank you to Marjorie Brody and the Monday Night Group, whose careful reading and insightful suggestions came at just the right time.

Thank you to all my family, my parents, and my brothers,

who are always in the mood to go out to dinner and celebrate. They say, "That's unbelievable," but they believe.

And finally, thank you, Fred. I could never have done this without you—your constant support, your patience, your tough love, and your unhesitating belief that I should be writing. This book belongs to you.

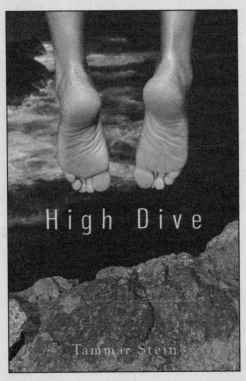